In Our Own Aboriginal Voice 2

With Thanks to

Anthology Selection Panel:

Chair–**Richard Van Camp,**
Author and member of the Dogrib (Tlicho) Nation,
Fort Smith

Sharon Buchanan,
Faculty & Student Support Services for Aboriginal Students,
Vancouver Island University – Shq'apthut

Patricia Geddes,
Student Engagement and Community Outreach Librarian,
Vancouver Island University

Daakwyii/Betty Knighton,
Culture & Youth Support Worker, Tsawalk Learning Centre

*With Special Thanks to Vancouver Island Regional Library for support and
partial sponsorship of prizes for the writing contest portion of this project.*

Partial proceeds of each book sold will be donated to
Tsawalk Learning Centre in Nanaimo, BC

Rebel Mountain Press-Nanoose Bay, BC, Canada

In Our Own Aboriginal Voice 2:

a collection of Indigenous authors and artists in Canada

Edited by Michael Calvert
Foreword by Edmund Metatawabin

Rebel Mountain Press, Nanoose Bay, BC

Edited by Michael Calvert, Mid-Island Métis Nation
Foreword by Edmund Metatawabin, Cree author and former Chief of Fort
Albany First Nation
Front Cover Art by Phillip Joe Jr., Quwutsun Tribes Reserve
Back Cover Illustration by Niki Watts, Cree
Cover Design & Layout, by Rebel Mountain Press

Library and Archives Canada Cataloguing in Publication

Title: In our own Aboriginal voice 2 : a collection of Indigenous authors and artists in
Canada /
  edited by Michael Calvert ; foreword by Edmund Metatawabin.
Other titles: In our own Aboriginal voice two | Collection of Indigenous authors and
artists in   Canada
Names: Calvert, Michael, 1968- editor. | Metatawabin, Edmund, 1947- writer of
foreword.
Description: First volume published under title: In our own Aboriginal voice : a
collection of Aboriginal writers and artists in BC.
Identifiers: Canadiana (print) 20190169451 | Canadiana (ebook) 20190169494 |
ISBN 9780994730299
  (softcover) | ISBN 9781775301912 (HTML)
Subjects: LCSH: Indigenous peoples—Canada—Literary collections. | CSH: Native
peoples—Canada—
  Literary collections. | CSH: Canadian literature (English)—Native authors. | CSH:
Native authors—Canada.
Classification: LCC PS8235.I6 I5 2019 | DDC C810.8/0897071—dc23

Printed & bound in Canada by Marquis Imprimeur Inc., Montreal, Quebec
ISBN 978-0-9947302-9-9 (bound)

Rebel Mountain Press—Nanoose Bay, BC, Canada
*We gratefully acknowledge that we are located on the traditional territory of the
Snaw-Naw-As First Nation.*

www.rebelmountainpress.com

DEDICATED TO – CONNIE FIFE

"When I sleep let it be in the arms of a poem"
- Connie Fife *(1961-2017)*

Born in Prince Albert, Saskatchewan on August 27, 1961, Connie was a survivor of the 60s Scoop. Her birth mother, Joy Rusic, daughter of Mildred Halcor and Horse Cook, was originally from Kinistino, SK. Joy is Métis, and Anglican. Connie was raised in Regina, Fiji, and England by an Anglican minister and his wife. It was a difficult childhood. Connie found solace in swimming and as a young athlete, in the beauty of the world, and in books. The works of Walt Whitman brought her great solace.

Connie was able to reconnect with her original family in recent years, through letters and phone calls, a rite of returning common for her generation. Although the 60s Scoop is today infamous, for decades it has been a hidden war. There will never be a finer Poet Laureate who can articulate the many-sidedness of this difficult historical period and the heart-breaking human realities ensconced in those two words: Sixties Scoop. At the time of her death, she was working on a new collection, 'Returned', which includes work from 2001 until February 3, 2017.

Connie's accomplishments were many, and her role in the literary life of Canada—writing and editing on behalf of Indigenous people and Lesbian, Gay, Bisexual, Transgender and Two Spirit people—was that of a courageous woman warrior and a pathfinder.

Her work has been included in *The Best Canadian Poetry In English* (2009), *An Anthology of Canadian Native Literature in English* (First, Second, & Third Editions), *Native Poetry in Canada: A Contemporary Anthology* (2001), *Outrage: Dykes and Bis Resist Homophobia* (1993), *Two Spirited People of First Nations* (1993), and *Piece of My Heart: Lesbian of Colour Anthology* (1991).

As editor or co-editor Connie brought three gatherings of writings by Indigenous people into publication. She received a fellowship from the Canadian Native Arts Foundation, and came west to study creative writing at the En'owkin International School of Writing in Penticton.

Her breakthrough anthology, *The Color of Resistance: A contemporary collection of writing by Aboriginal women* (Sister Vision, 1993) was her second published book. She received a grant from CUSO in support of this project. This beautiful book stands the test of time. It is described by Sister Vision Press as "A powerful collection of works in response to 500 years of colonization, and the worldwide celebrations marking the anniversary of European invasion."

Connie's books of poetry, no less than the volumes of work edited for and with others, demonstrate a person of significant insight and literary gifts. Poetry was her vehicle of desire, observation, affirmation, protest, resistance, and celebration.

In 2000, Connie was one of four Indigenous artists to receive the one time Prince and Princess Edward prize in Aboriginal Literature in recognition of her contribution both in our community, and to Canada as a whole. This prize was Canada's wedding gift to Prince Edward and Princess Sophie. In its press release, the Canada Council for the Arts described her contributions: "Poet and writer Connie Fife has inspired and influenced many emerging Aboriginal writers. Her pen is fearless and she has consistently used the power of the word to break through the barriers of injustice and intolerance."

Over the years, Connie sat on many juries for book prizes, arts grants, and literary awards, including both Saskatchewan and Governor General Awards. She participated in Indigenous literary gatherings in many of the major cities in Canada. Connie lived for ten years in Regina, SK, at the beginning of her life, and for ten years at the end of her life in Haines Junction, YT. Her son Russell was born March 8, 1980 in Toronto, ON. She also lived in Winnipeg, Vancouver, Victoria, and Nanaimo, involving herself in activism and community support work in every place.

In her final years, Connie was delighted to spend time with her grandchildren, Cameron Andrew Cole Fife (b. Nov 8, 2011) and Hayley Margaret Ann Fife (b. Feb 19, 2014), the children of her son Russell Fife and Glenda Miersch. Her Haines Junction family also included Glenda's older children, her mother, and her ex-partner's/family friend Julie Moore. Connie relied upon her family as she battled with health issues and sought peace and productivity in the world. Her generosity and kindness are well remembered by many who knew her.

~by Joanne Arnott

Contents

Foreword

By Edmund Metatawabin

Former Chief of Fort Albany First Nation, and author of *Up Ghost River: A Chief's Journey Through the Turbulent Waters of Native History*, with Alexandra Shimo, (2015, Penguin Random House); Finalist for the 2014 Governor General's Literary Award for Non-Fiction.

After anger
I sing.
To the wind I sing.
I sing to the four directions, I sing for my life
I hear, I can smell, I can think, feel, and I see
I can choose to sing for life.
I am free! I feel free! I must be free!?

Birds will sing first thing in the morning. At the end of the day, the birds will once again sing. They may have lost many members to predators. Poisonous air may have caused others to fall from the sky. Life and death are part of life. The circle closes. That is accepted.

Like birds, we must remind ourselves that we have much to be grateful for. We also lose some of our members to predators; those refined ones with suits who follow protocol, the rough ones on meager existence, and even our own pretenders in borrowed clothing.

They, the predators, have learned from the best. Biblical words uttered in shadowy, dark halls as the familiar shuffle of uncertain, anxious steps get closer to your protected shell of flimsy blankets. In vain you are trying to be invisible and noiseless. You close your body, but the formative brain copies and formats the imposed file. As the steps fade away, the stain left cannot be removed even with pins and needles on unfeeling skin. Numerous accusing eyes follow your every move, nightly trauma exposed for all to see.

You were just a child. You were innocent. Like a bird attempting to finish a broken song, confusion came with the beautiful sunrise versus your suffering inner soul. "It's a beautiful sunrise of reddish purple on blue backdrop so why do I feel an anguished pain in my heart, looking to spill uncontrollably?"

Then we become adults. But, we retain the 'ward' title. We are free to do whatever we want "if the Minister so wishes." Whatever sin we committed in the past, whatever atrocity we were part of, we now are in debt for it. The registered Indians, like registering for residential school, are inmates of the Canadian total institution under the heading "The Indian Act." Initiated by the Papal Bull (policy), the Church (mid-1500s) allowed Portugal to invade northern Africa, and since the Indigenous population were not Christian, they had no ownership title and the lands and resources could be taken freely. Jump forward in Canada and the papal policy still influences Canadian Law and its perception of Indigenous ownership and rights to land.

This book echoes the voices of those who wish for a better situation for themselves and their community the world over. The elusive search for autonomy, although given to oneself, is not within policy in Canada. Canada says, "You do not have standing!" The message seems to be that court and justice belongs to Canadians only! Those of us who have a band number (a registered Indian number) or who identify with Turtle Island, cannot claim such privilege. We ask together, what exactly is the relationship between the Indigenous population and this country? Are we in the way?

"Disconnection is what I feel," says an author. Another points to the policy that resulted *"in massive loss of language and culture,"* another mourns family breakdown—*"That was the last time I saw him"*; language loss—*"I can't remember my language"*; homelessness—*"there were a lot of people shuffling around."*

As children in residential school, we know what it is like to be *"starved of affection."* We know what it is like to be alone, to be afraid, wondering what horror tomorrow will bring. The feeling of isolation is thousands of years old. It was there when an old, old ancestor lost a mate through war, accident, or time. From then on, they would have to cope with life's many trials on their own, without familiar support. Today, as we unceremoniously desert our children, spouse, kin, or community, do we not consider their fear of coping on their own? *"Where is my shadow, to shade me from my foes and insulate us from the harsh winds?"*

However, after five hundred years of colonization, 'not one Indian turned white!' We are still who we are! We may have lost our song, but remember, it's only forgotten! A few more offerings and we'll get them back. We will sing to our grandchildren in the morning because there is no longer anyone to stop us.

The word Reconciliation was invented by the government and Catholic Church, as an act of contrition, for being caught for the abuses inside residential schools. We could not, however, sense any contrition on their part. It was a good word, but the Indian Act stayed the same. No one made any effort to change it!

In an effort to remind ourselves as unique Indigenous people, Reclamation refers to the need to recover neglected traditions and beliefs thousands of years old. This is not to say we will change ideas to meet ours, but rather, we will provide choice to the young people about what to believe in.

Mandela and Paul (of the Apostles), gave up their freedom to retain what they strongly believed was patrimony from a higher source. Confined, defined to be refined, they held steadfast to their beliefs. Inheritance is an accepted concept. "What did your dad leave you?" or "What skills did your mother leave you with?" are words expressed to the survivors of departed parents. We have the same responsibility as Mandela and Paul to cherish and protect patrimony.

"We shall overcome," expresses this desire to carry tradition to the next generation. We would like it to happen quickly, but evolution has other ideas. Patience will make sense and this is where the teachings of our ancestors come in to help us. Change does not happen quickly. Climate change started in the 1940s and will continue to plod on until the next century as the autumn of time takes over.

In the meantime, we will laugh. We will cry. We will accept our time and prepare the way for change. We will overcome. We will seek to attain rightful heritage. Our example of resilience will be taken over by the next generation who will raise their voices to the wind and sing . . . *'ah wiya nah ne-o, kana wi-ana wi-ana-neo. 'For someone lost in their own land,'* we will say *'the morning prayer,'* get back on *'the red road,'* to proudly claim, *'I am a survivor!'* As today's young children *'are looking for prayers,'* we can be the ones to teach them.

Like a bird that sings for a new day, we will, after the song, prepare our community for the arrival of *'those that are not yet born.'* We will re-kindle the legacy left to us by our Elders: "if you're careful to preserve it right, you'll have it for years to come."

The poets and short-story writers who contributed here for our enjoyment leave us with the message that you are known; someone knows you exist, "*I no longer must fear that I am alone.*" We carry the gift of life. We share in that experience with the spirits of nature. With their singing words, painting pictures in your heart, they insist that your life is acknowledged. Your experience is being recorded. Let's all make the most of it! Enjoy the book.

– Edmund

Introduction

By Michael Calvert, Editor
Mid-Island Métis Nation

I'll begin by saying how honoured I am to have worked with each of the contributors in this book and all of those who were a part of its production. I'd also like to acknowledge that the work of editing this book, at least on my end, was done on the traditional unceded territory of the Snuneymuxw people. I am grateful to be a visitor on their traditional land and to do the rewarding work I do here.

The inspiring collection of work within these pages combines prolific, established Aboriginal writers and poets like the late Connie Fife, to whom this book is dedicated, and Joanne Arnott, with up-and-coming authors, poets, and artists, all of whom will leave you captivated, while rendering a clearer understanding of today's Indigenous voice in all its range. From Elders, and from artists, poets, and storytellers, young and old, exploration of Indigenous identity is woven throughout the book you hold in your hands. The connection to thousands of years of culture and tradition remains strong for some, while, for others, this connection to identity remains severed and impalpable.

The power emanating from the verse and story contained herein, from these writers and poets across Canada, issues forth from their searching through the rubble of hundreds of years of colonization and forced assimilation. There is a yearning to understand the hows and whys of what has—or for most, what hasn't—been passed down to them. Here, they've put voice to the emotions that tear through us when we are left with questions that so few have the answers to. Questions about where we come from, who we are, and where we're going. These are questions about the journeys we must take alone and those we must, as we are all related and living on the same Mother Earth, take together. But before we can understand reconciliation, we must hear the truths.

Whether filled with joy, curiosity, or anger, these are the voices, these are the truths we must hear and acknowledge if we are to move forward together in a good way, in a healing way.

As Edward Metatawabin offers in his foreword, "we will overcome" and "our example of resilience will be taken over by the next generation who will raise their voices to the wind and sing…"

Indeed.

Marsee,

Michael Calvert

Jerry Smaaslet
Carrier Sikanni Clan

Locked Up: An Inmate's Journey back to the Red Road

Editor's note:
(A segment of this story first appeared in volume one of In Our Own Aboriginal Voice.*)*
Taken from their isolated reserve in Fort Ware, BC by Canada Welfare during the 60s Scoop, the Smaaslet brothers, Jerry and Ernie, were relocated to white foster care in Prince George, BC.

Notes from Social Worker report (1967-71):
"The foster parents, Mr. and Mrs. M, think both boys are able to be assimilated into white society. "[The boys] have almost been assimilated into white society (as opposed to being integrated), i.e. they have learned values, e.g. placing value on "things," cleanliness, values which were absent from their Indian environment."
"Mr. and Mrs. M run a fairly strict household."
"Mrs. M thinks stealing is inbred in Indians."
"Jerry's self-image may be suffering. Mrs. M again called him a no-good Indian."
"The boys are well fed and well provided for. The only thing the [foster] home seems to lack is emotional warmth and affection."

I am a casualty of the 60s Scoop. I was only four when my brother, Ernie, and I were taken from my mother on the reserve and placed with a white foster family who had three boys of their own. We were forced to live in this alien environment, vastly different from the family and nation where we should have been raised. The welfare system knew we were mistreated and abused, but did nothing to help. The foster parents were very strict and their beatings were constant. There was a complete lack of affection. I was made to run around the farm shoeless. I'd round-up the cows for milking through fields full of sharp twigs and thorns, the ground damp and cold with rain and frost. It was normal to be sent to bed without any supper, forced to kneel in a corner on hard, dried white beans, and locked in the gravel-floored basement with no light. I always felt safer out in the fields surrounded by the cows and dangerous wildlife than in the misery of my foster home. To make matters even worse, by the time I turned six years old, the oldest son began to molest me—a memory I had buried deep inside.

My foster brother would warn me not to tell anyone about what he did to me. I remember there were boxes of apples under the stairs. He took one apple out and made me bite it, then threatened to show his parents if I told, which would have resulted in a strapping with a thick strap from a horse's harness. At this young age, I already felt the urge to hurt these people back for the hurt they caused me.

I showed very little interest in school, so I had poor grades. I was often into mischief, getting into fights and bullying the other children. Like an abandoned wild animal, I was left to struggle on my own to live, and my survival instincts kicked in.

By age eight or nine, I was feeling much stronger and started to use this strength in an unnatural, dominant fashion. In school, I never felt included; festive events, social events, and sporting events were not for me. But there was one thing at school I was good at. It was called King of the Castle. When snow piled high on the sports fields, the object of the game was for every child to climb to the top of the snow hill. The one who was able to throw the other children off and stay at the top the longest was called the King of the Castle. I always threw the most kids from the top. I didn't care how high we were, or who got hurt—being King of the Castle was all that mattered. It gave me an exhilarating sense of power to become this alpha male. This alpha male wolf became one of many masks I learned to hide behind. It was relief from the horrible fear and darkness I experienced in the foster home. I was filled with anger, and soon I became the one who was feared by many.

One day, a taxi drove up to the farm. I and the other children were out at the woodpile. A native lady got out of the cab, holding onto the top of the cab with a cane for support. I couldn't hear what was being said, but the native lady was gesturing with her head and arms while my foster mom shook her head, indicating no. Later, after the women had driven away in the taxi, my foster parents shared that it was just drunken Indians looking for someone. They had told her there were no Indians living on the farm. Much later, when I was fifteen and had reconnected with my biological mother, she told me that it was, in fact, her in the cab that day. She also revealed that I had biological brothers and sisters, grandparents, aunts, uncles—a whole family that my deceitful foster parents lied about and told me I didn't have.

I lived with my foster family on the farm for over a decade, between the ages of four and fourteen. I still remember the beatings, some so brutal that I had to soak in a tub for hours afterward, or that I had to miss a few weeks of school because the bruising was so bad. My fear had turned to anger that boiled within—someone would have to pay for my pain.

Then quite unexpectedly on an Easter weekend when I was about fourteen, my brother and I were allowed to spend time with our biological mother. We were very excited to be driven into the city of Prince George to meet our mother, and, for the first time, to meet our biological sister, too. I felt free being away from the farm, but the damage had been done. It was a strange encounter; they were both strangers to me. Yet I felt uplifted because I was free from the abuse on the farm. I felt like the alpha male wolf was left to roam amongst sheep.

I still blame my biological father for where I ended up, for abandoning my mom with her debilitating condition. She believed I would receive a better upbringing in foster care, something that she couldn't fully offer because of her handicap. When my brother and I began spending time with our mom, I was a young teenager on the verge of manhood and the alpha male wolf was gaining strength. I didn't trust my biological mother; I defied her and everyone around me. Like in the schoolyard years before, I was the King of the Castle. I set out into a brand new world, learning to survive at all cost.

The system, setup to protect me, had failed. Children need a healthy environment, proper nurturing, safety, education in social skills, guidance in turning harmful emotions into positive ones, and first and foremost, children need a loving family. My brother and I needed a father to teach us hunting and fishing skills so we could provide for ourselves and those around us. We needed our mom to give us a loving family life, to teach us social skills and compassion.

As I grew into manhood, I became skilled at putting on new and different masks. I also found my dad, who was living in a pay-by-themonth hotel with his new partner and her daughter. He was a complete stranger to me, though, and we could not generate an emotional bond. During this time I lived with my mom in a hotel, and I spent my time in the local bars. The alpha male in me began to use his new found strength and would lash out physically when felt threatened or cornered. My friends noticed and tried to hide their fear, but I could see it in their eyes.

The violence got so bad that welfare had to send my brother and me to Fort Ware to live with my grandmother on the reserve, the Carrier Sikanni Nation. I didn't even know where Fort Ware was, only that it is so isolated it is only accessible by air. Fort Ware is actually one of the most isolated communities in BC. From the plane, we had a long walk to my grandmother's house where we eventually met the rest of our biological family: our grandfather, uncles and aunties, and another biological brother.

Child welfare, in their great wisdom, thought it better that I be isolated away from city life. They did not realize it was like sending me into a great wasps' nest. It was exactly my kind of environment—a reserve of turmoil, drinking, fighting, and everything unruly. The alpha male in me flourished. I took on all adversaries and adversities that came my way. I was in fights, stabbed, shot at, chased with an axe. People were sniffing gas, stealing each other's home brew, and it was an everyday occurrence because there were no cops around. There were good times, too—lots of parties—but most people never knew much about my past and rough upbringing. Here I was, a young buck, a full-status Indian on reserve, and it was a very different world for me. I didn't know how to hunt or shoot, I didn't know how to handle myself in the bush or camp, and I didn't even understand my native tongue—I didn't know squat. I was a total greenhorn, one very lost warrior among his own people.

I still had so much rage. I felt no remorse or empathy. I told no one on the reserve about my past and my childhood pain. I was still the alpha male wolf amongst the sheep, even though these were my own people. Eventually, my uncle took my brother and me out spring trapping. He taught me how to stalk moose and deer, and how to move through the forest. Yet, I started drinking again; I got back into home brew, smoking-up, sniffing gas, and fighting. I stopped going to school and took up firefighting in the bush and other odd jobs to make money. I got into building houses for the band. We had no amenities then; no electricity, only woodstoves for heat and cooking, no indoor plumbing, and we had to pack our own water from the river.

I became stronger. I was constantly in the bush fighting fires. I also climbed many mountains, hunted lots of different game, and soon the "greenhorn" excelled in his new environment. But one huge issue still haunted me. The ever-present darkness of my past was still buried deep inside of me.

In 1980, I lost my mother to alcohol poisoning; the alcohol killed her liver. She died in Prince George, and we buried her on the reserve. I felt a lot of rage over losing her—because I wasn't there for her.

Around this time, in my twenties, the assaults began and charges started getting laid against me. I even assaulted the chief, which resulted in six months in a provincial jail. When I was released and returned to my reserve with even more rage inside of me, I ended up almost killing my chief and was sentenced to five years in a federal prison. Just like every other prisoner, I jumped through their hoops, showing them what they wanted to see to gain early release. But halfway through my five-year sentence the worst happened. My brother Ernie, my rock who held my hand through the punishment and torturous times in foster care, had died, taken from me by cancer. I wanted to attend his memorial and funeral, but I learned that he had actually died six months earlier. I was furious at my family for not telling me sooner, and I was even madder at the chief. I thought about whom I could retaliate against—who would pay.

When I finally got out on parole, I decided to go back to the reserve to visit my brother's grave. I purchased a duffle bag and filled it with liquor and drugs. At Ernie's gravesite, I took out a mickey of whiskey and for every drink I took, I poured one on top of his grave. My brother had always been there to pull me off someone and calm me down before anyone was seriously hurt. And now here I was, with a bunch of liquor and coke chasers, feeling all alone. The one person I had relied on was gone. Memories of the abuse in that foster home weighed heavy on my mind, and I knew I had climbed a few more notches up the dark road.

I eventually left the reserve and Fort Ware and returned to Prince George where I entered into an abusive situation similar to my foster home experiences. I was now using hard drugs, cocaine and heroin, for months on end. I overdosed four times and nearly died. My new circle of friends from the bars didn't care who I was or where I came from; they didn't judge me nor I them. I was always in pretty rough shape from the drugs. Eventually, I met a woman and began a very volatile, unstable relationship fuelled by cocaine and heroin. We constantly fought about drugs. Many bad and stupid things happened to me in life because of alcohol and drugs. Regretfully, I made a lot of very bad decisions that led the system to slap me with the label of D.O., or dangerous offender—a label that always carries a longer and stiffer sentence for Natives.

I want to acknowledge what life-givers and brothers have gone through in the Residential School System designed to break and take the Indian out of them. And all the First Nations people affected by the 60s Scoop, with families separated and children stolen from their biological families and placed in foster care with different ethnicities. To all the brothers and sisters out there who buried the pain and hurt as I did, I say: Trust me, if you don't do something about it, it will eventually ruin you—your relationships, your future, everything. That is why I am still in prison, even now, serving a life sentence. It will not go away just because you bury or ignore it. It is time for you to step forward and start believing in yourself. It is time for you to be heard. Stop and think about why you are always getting angry. Your reactions rub off on your children. Bring out your inner child, your true feelings. Ho-Ho, my brothers and sisters, I hope my story touches you.

Ironically, it was in prison where I finally learned to be who I really am. In prison, I worked closely with Elders and took many Aboriginal-based programs to open myself up and help heal my troubled childhood. One program I completed, High Intensity Aboriginal Substance Abuse, was very interesting. With the help of the facilitator, our group was able to go back into our hurtful past to share the pain that comes with losing one's identity, and to use tools already within us as stepping stones in our journey down the Red Road. One Elder who stood out for me as a powerful influence is Mr. Ken Pruden. He has always been there for me, offering encouragement even when I was struggling through schooling, always coaxing me onto completion. He believed in me; he saw things in me that I myself didn't. He saw me as a person who could succeed. I thank Mr. Pruden for being there and making me feel like a human being again and not a prisoner of the penal system.

Other programs that really helped me were Aboriginal High Intensity

Family Violence, and In Search of Your Warrior. I have gone into detail about these programs in the first volume of *In Our Own Aboriginal Voice,* but to summarize, these three programs gave me many strong and useful tools to help deal with my childhood issues and gain insight into my behaviours to reduce the risk of violence. With the help of the Elders and these programs, I was finally able to let my inner child surface—and I listened. I rock him, cry with him, hold him, nurture him, and love him the way I should have been loved from the beginning, so long ago. Learning to treat myself with kindness, care, love, and respect is the only way to heal, learn, and grow.

I have changed my life around as I walk the Red Road. And I am proud to say that I have recently completed Grade 12, something that I never expected to do in my life. I have also recently been transferred

Jerry Smaaslet photo

from maximum security to the healing village Kwikwexwelhp. I am Fire Keeper for sweat ceremonies and keeping my brothers—who are each on their individual journey of discovery and healing on the Red Road—safe in our healing village, taking part in powerful spiritual rituals of the Medicine Wheel teachings. I acknowledge who I am now and what I have accomplished, rather than who I was then.

My healing has not been easy. It is filled with questions, confusion, and inner struggles. It includes denial, suffering, moving one step forward and two steps back. Still, I journey on. My spirit warrior becomes my champion, my own cheering section that makes me believe there is a purpose, a reason to go on, so I do. I make mistakes and fall back into old patterns, get angry at myself, and go on. My spirit warrior gives me the strength to carry on. I do it, also, for my son from my past relationship.

Hopefully, through my experiences, others may recognize something of themselves and gain insights into their own struggles. I encourage all to open up to the Elders because they are the most precious resource we have, and they are available to all. I am in humble adoration of the Elders and the other people who have helped assist me on my journey of healing. I humble myself before them, and with my heartfelt gratitude, I say, "All My Relations."

I want to share the powerful message of hope and truth to give us all strength to survive. I acknowledge the other surviving adults of the foster care system. This is our story.

As I step out of the darkness of my past and into the sunlight of my future, my heart truly soars. First and foremost, the journey of a thousand miles begins with one step. So step forward, my brothers and sisters.

~ All My Relations ~

Drum made and painted by
Jerry Smaaslet

Darlene McIntosh
Elder - Lheidli T'enneh Nation

Sacred Ceremony of Smudging

As I stand facing east
watching the sun come up . . .

I acknowledge and give thanks for what this new day will bring . . .

Creator put the Sacred Smudge Bowl in my hands
to be present in the moment . . .

Using my breath . . . I begin to connect with myself and Mother Earth ...

Using the eagle feather, I pull the sacred burning smudge over my body,
cleansing my thoughts, my emotions and all that clings to me
I am in prayer to my Creator . . .

The Ancestors are here with me . . . supporting me as I call out to the
Grandfathers and Grandmothers to be with me always . . .

I pray to my Ancestors to guide and support me throughout this day . . .

I ask Creator to take my burdens, my sadness, and feelings of being stuck
I am deep . . . deep in prayer as I immerse my whole being in the energy
of what is taking place . . .

I sink into the sweet-smelling earth of the Mother who grounds me
into today . . .
Reaching for the sky, I give thanks to Creator who gives me life.

The rainbow of colours saturate my eyes, and I know Creator has
heard me . . .

I start my day in a good way . . .
Bringing all my energies into balance and harmony . . .

This . . . I am grateful for . . .

Snachailya Creator, Mother Earth,

and all my relations

Photography by Darlene McIntosh

Sheena Robinson
Heiltsuk Nation

Saving Cedar Saving Me

Pulling bark from fallen cedars
in a clear cut,
like skinning animals
weeks after they've been shot.
No spirit left to pray to,
just pulling skin from corpses.
"Sorry," I whisper. "Thank you."
But nobody hears.
The sea is too far.

masks, rattles, benches, cradles

The warp and weft of my
wandering mind
is an insult to the hands
which spent hours weaving,
plaiting soaked cedar strips,
minds focused,
eyes not wavering,
teeth worn down from chewing
bark and roots.
Not thinking, just doing.

hats, mats, blankets, baskets

On the ocean I wince
from the inconvenience
of the fishing rod
digging into my hip
and the two hundred feet of line
I must reel in
with arms too used to typing.

The spine of the snapper
frightens me, and I
pass off my catch,
heart in my throat.

planks, posts, combs, floats

My ancestors laugh
and rub their arms,
remembering rowing or
paddling miles to the edges of
Heiltsuk territory,
fishing line made of twined branches,
hooks carved from the knots of hemlock,
fingers blistering as they jig,
muscles burning like my skin.

canoes, ropes, nets, line

I pick huckleberries right-handed
one at a time,
dropping them into a plastic jug
that I grasp with my left.
No basket hanging around this neck.
Rattled by each snap of a branch,
but the bears have left this growth
for me, a pity offering
for someone lost in her own land,
trying to find home.

whistles, paddles, totems, coffins

Eliot White-Hill, Kwulasultun
Snuneymuxw First Nation

Waves Crashing Upon the Shore

The waves crashed upon the shore, over and over again. The same rhythmic pattern that followed the ebb and flow of the tide. A movement that has always repeated itself and always will. As the waves flowed in they would talk to each other.

Where is everyone? they asked.

They aren't here yet, they answered.

They will be here though.

Living things were not yet inhabiting the world, but the waves knew they were on their way. The waves were excited because of this. The sand on the beach was excited too, as well as the winds, and also the beings who would join them from the spiritual realm beyond the horizon. The world was busy, and, in this place, there was much work to do.

There is going to be so much hurt, the sand said to the sea. *And it won't go away so easily,* the wind chimed in. *That is why we help. To cleanse the wounds, both material and immaterial, together,* the sea responded.

Ho ho, called the beings beyond the horizon.

Ho ho, the world responded.

Ho ho, called the waves, crashing upon the shore.

It had been decided that this place, where the three physical worlds met with the spiritual, would be a place of cleansing. A place of movement, out and away from the state of being hurt.

~

I sat at my usual table in the café. I had already ordered my coffee, and the owner, without a word, delivered it to my table. A quick nod was the only acknowledgement necessary. I had never shared more than a few words with him. I don't think anyone had. He was a solemn, middle-aged man whose presence within the café was indistinguishable from that of the clock or the mugs lining the shelves. It seemed to me that this person did not exist in any place but within the confines of this café.

It was a very average café, situated within a commercial development along the waterfront that had appeared at some point within the past half-century. It was quiet inside, for the owner did not play any sort of music. The steady whir and grinding of the machines and their operator often dominated the auditory stage of the place, but in the lulls, one could hear the sound of waves crashing upon the shore, coming from just outside.

I came here every day. I had long since lost track of how many weeks or months it had been. It was part of my routine; my ritual. Every day, between the hours of two and six, this was where I existed, and my presence within this place was broken only by short moments wherein I stepped outside to smoke a cigarette, which I did precisely four times each day.

Aside from those breaks, I was invariably sitting at my table, with headphones blaring music, poring over the internet from my laptop. Any sort of social interaction I could possibly need was at arm's reach from this position. Through my patronage to this café, I fulfilled my necessary social role and obligations; through it I served my purpose as a cog within both the social and economic machines.

Today was different. I was aware of it from the moment I entered the café. It was as though the proportions of the space had misaligned, the ceiling too high, the floor too low, the lights shone piercingly, the windows seemed like gaping holes in the walls, the seat creaked, the tablecloth stuck to my arms, and something had come loose inside one of the coffee machines and it clanked violently. This space was not the café I knew. Empirically, this was certainly the same place where I had spent each day, but the phenomena portrayed something entirely different. Something had come loose within the café, exposing those within to the elements.

~

The sun had yet to rise. The sky was a deep, dark blue. A group of people walked down the beach. They walked solemnly. They did not speak amongst themselves, but, silently, their thoughts called out to each other.

It is time.
Will we be forgiven?
We have taken too much from the world.
Our attachment to this place has caused great harm.

A mist had begun to form, and the dim outlines of the stars were visible through it. The birds were not yet awake; the only sound was that of the waves crashing upon the shore.

When the people reached the water, the eldest among them instructed the rest on what to do. One by one, they disrobed and waded into the water, always facing forward, never looking back. They bathed themselves, wading deep into the ocean before receding toward the shore, washing their bodies all the while. They repeated this process three more times before leaving the water.

Once each had completed the act, they gathered and sat in the sand. The salty water dried quickly upon their skin. The eldest stood, addressing the world:

"We have come here seeking forgiveness, seeking cleansing, seeking the help to find strength within ourselves to begin our journey away from this place."

The eldest paused, preparing.

"We have strayed far from the path of our Ancestors. We have overstayed our welcome here. Our presence and attachment here, for so long, led to us taking more than necessary. This has caused great harm and pain to the world around us—to the natural beings. We recognize this and are ashamed. We come begging forgiveness. We hope to return things to the way they are meant to be, the way that it has been for generations innumerable."

The rest of them stood, alongside the eldest, and together they waited.

A long time passed. To the people, it felt like many, many hours, perhaps even days had gone by, but the sun still had yet to rise.

A voice came bubbling up through the sand, it entered each of them through their feet, went up past their legs, and settled itself somewhere within the very core of their beings.

Thank you, it said; the water, the sand, the winds, and all of the beings spoke as one. *Thank you for sharing your bodily energies with us. Thank you for remembering the way to open yourselves, passed down through your teachings. Thank you for being humble and aware, I am proud of you for that, my grandchildren.*

The voice turned grave.

You have indeed caused great harm to the world. The smaller beings, whom you have preyed upon and stockpiled in excess, are diminished. They have left this place to rejuvenate themselves. You took more than you needed. You stayed when you should have gone. You became stuck, deeply stuck. The beings in the world are hurting because of you. They are not angry, rather they are sad that you have become this way.

The people listened silently.

You shall be forgiven, but you must leave this place and linger no longer. I will help bring you to the next place. You will not be able to return here. Not for a very long time.

The people felt the presence dissipate; they said nothing but raised their arms in gratitude and acknowledgement. The sun peeked its face over the mountains.

"It is time," they said.

They left the beach, returning to their home. When they got there, they disassembled the house. They dug up the house posts and burned them. By the time the four posts had turned from ember to ash, the people were gone.

Ho ho, called the ashes, in the pit.

Ho ho, called the people, from beyond the horizon.

Ho ho, called the waves, crashing upon the shore.

~

I put my headphones on, trying to block out what was happening to the world around me; the music droned louder, and my brow furrowed as my eyes attempted to burn a hole through the laptop screen. I looked desperately to the coffee cup for answers; it looked back at me, but had none.

Finally, I stood and stormed out the door, lighting a cigarette in the process. I went to the railing overlooking the water and hung my arms upon it.

The waves were overwhelming; they rolled in tumultuously, unending. They were looking at me. Judging me, with a million eyes in the foam. I glared back, trying to understand their voice that sang out against the shore.

"Excuse me," said a voice.

I dropped my cigarette, looking about, confused.

"Your phone is ringing."

It was the owner, standing at the open door.

I stepped back inside and checked my phone; a missed call notification appeared. It was from a one-eight-hundred number, likely some telemarketer. I sat down, took a deep breath, and put my headphones back on.

Everything was back to normal.

The waves outside continued crashing upon the shore.

Ho ho, they called; but it fell upon deaf ears.

~

What of those who cannot hear our voice, those who are unable to ask for help?
We cannot force them to ask, to come looking. We can only be present.
We must wait until they are ready.
Ho ho.

Art by
Phil Joe

Connie Fife
Cree

Sunday
(Originally published in Arc Poetry Magazine 84, October 2017)

Pasted on inner church walls crucifixion pierced original sin.
Who i was became petal then bloom of lily.
Palm cross passed from hand to hand.
Cold floor, echo of dry cough.
Untruth, ingredient of fiction not poetry.
I imagined the stretching Saskatchewan river.
Its ferocity spoke of home.
My displacement pulled under,
pew and cross slid down eroded embankment,
dragged downstream out of earshot and sight.

Dennis Saddleman
Nlaka'pamux Nation, Coldwater Band

Monster, a Residential School Experience

I hate you residential school
I hate you
You're a monster
A huge, hungry monster
Built with steel bones
Built with cement flesh
You're a monster
Built to devour
Innocent Native children
You're a cold-hearted monster
Cold as your cement floors
You have no love
No gentle atmosphere
Your ugly face grooved with red bricks, your monster eyes glare
From grimy windows
Monster eyes so evil
Monster eyes watching
Terrified children
Cower with shame

I hate you, residential school, I hate you
You're a slimy monster
Oozing in the shadows of my past
Go away. Leave me alone
You're following me, following me wherever I go
You're in my dreams, in my memories
Go away, Monster, go away
I hate you, you're following me
I hate you, residential school, I hate you
You're a monster with a huge, watery mouth of double doors
Your wide mouth took me

Your yellow-stained teeth chewed
The Indian out of me
Your teeth crunched my language
Ground my rituals and my traditions, your taste buds became bitter
When you tasted my red skin
You swallowed me with disgust
Your face wrinkled when you
Tasted my strong pride

I hate you, residential school, I hate you
You're a monster
Your throat muscles forced me
Down to your stomach
Your throat muscles squeezed my happiness
Squeezed my dreams
Squeezed my Native voice
Your throat became clogged with my sacred spirit
You coughed and you choked
For you cannot withstand my
Spiritual songs and dances

I hate you, residential school, I hate you—you're a monster
Your stomach became upset every time I wet my bed, your stomach
Rumbled with anger
Every time I fell asleep in church
Your stomach growled at me every time I broke the school rules,
Your stomach was full
Then you burped, you felt satisfied
You rubbed your belly, and you didn't care, you didn't care how you
Ate up my Native culture
You didn't care if you were messy
If you were a piggy
You didn't care as long as you ate up my *"Indianness"*

I hate you, residential school, I hate you
You're a monster
Your veins clotted with cruelty and torture

KAMLOOPS
INDIAN RESIDENTIAL
A.D. SCHOOL 1923

Your blood poisoned with loneliness and despair
Your heart was cold, it pumped fear into me
I hate you, residential school, I hate you
You're a monster
Your intestines turned me into foul entrails
Your anus squeezed me
Squeezed my confidence
Squeezed my self respect
Your anus squeezed
Then you dumped me
Dumped me without parental skills
Without life skills
Dumped me without any form of character
Without individual talents
Without a hope for success
I hate you, residential school, I hate you
You're a monster
You dumped me in the toilet then you flushed out my good nature,
My personalities
I hate you, residential school, I hate you

Thirty-three years later
I rode my Chevy Pony to Kamloops
From the highway, I saw the monster
My gawd! The monster is still alive
I hesitated—I wanted to drive on
But something told me to stop
I parked in front of the residential school
In front of the monster
The monster saw me, and it stared at me
The monster saw me, and I stared back
Neither of us said anything for a long time
Finally, with a lump in my throat
I said, "Monster, I forgive you."
The monster broke into tears
The monster cried and cried
His huge shoulders shook

He motioned for me to come forward
He asked me to sit on his lappy stairs
The monster spoke
"You know I didn't like my government father
I didn't like my catholic church mother
I'm glad the Native people adopted me
They took me as one of their own
They fixed me up, repaired my mouth of double doors, washed my
Window eyes with cedar and fir boughs
And they cleansed me with sage and sweetgrass
Now my good spirit lives
The Native people let me stay on their land
They could have burnt me you know; instead, they let me live
So people can come here and restore or learn about their culture,"
Said the monster.
"I'm glad the Native people gave me another chance. I'm glad,
Dennis, you gave me another chance."
The monster smiled
I stood up, and I told the monster I must go
Ahead of me is my life. My people are waiting for me
I was at the door of my Chevy Pony
The monster spoke, "Hey, you forgot something"
I turned around, I saw a ghost child running down the cement steps,
It ran toward me, and it entered
My body
I looked over to the monster. I was surprised
I wasn't looking at a monster anymore
I was looking at an old school in my heart. I thought
This is where I earned my diploma of survival
I was looking at an old residential school who
Became my Elder of my memories
I was looking at a tall building with four stories
Stories of hope
Stories of dreams
Stories of renewal
And stories of tomorrow.

Michelle Sylliboy
L'nuk (Mi'kmaq)

Sprinkling pixy dust

Sprinkling pixy dust
into an unknown mind
while writing without a broom
allows you to experience a moment where emptiness must occur
in order to create

breathe work
breathe work

oxygen channels
simultaneously
gazing
across from a room
we all want to occupy

as we notify
our spirit
to graciously take over

undulating with calmness
fire crackles a song
between an embodiment of torment
sacrificing on purpose for a mere second

all the while
infusion takes over rumblings of
a concentrated effort signifying
death and life a congruent gone astray

leaving the mind
to wonder

was she just a speck of dust
transformed to live between the dandelions of misaligned fields of
a significant malcontented misinformed human being who mumbles
between meals just to make a statement

it's not what you think
she inhales with a breath
that shames no one
laying underneath a table
despite no after shocks

sun rises
moon wobbles
stars aligned
let us not misinterpret
anymore

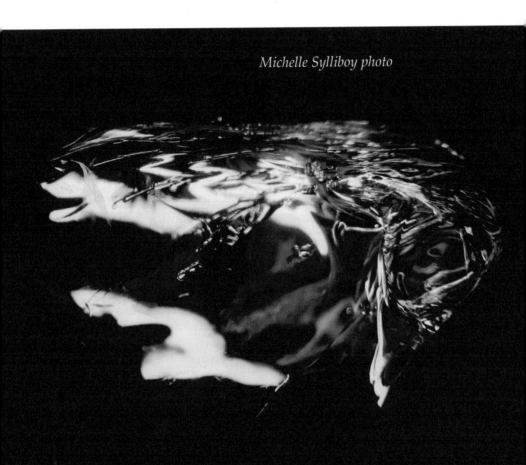

Michelle Sylliboy photo

Myles Neufeld
Skeetchestn Indian Band

Little Fox

I sprinted, my feet bleeding from the sharp rocks and twigs in this forest, and my hands cut from the lashing from only moments before. And while the fear kept me going, the exhaustion and hunger tried to weigh me down. I heard them closing in, the demons in my head and the teachers chasing me, and I kept running until the lights dimmed in the distance and the moon hid my tracks.

I looked around, still fearing what they might do if they caught me; I found a damp, rotting, fallen log and crawled in, keeping silent even as the bugs crawled on my skin, past my ears, and into my hair.

I heard footsteps near, and I stifled my cries as I felt things bite into skin. While trying to hold back the pain, my crying instantly stopped as the memories of bleach, and the burn of it on my skin, filled my senses.

"Katy!" they called out, with voices far too calm as they walked by.

They were trying to trick me. I knew they were because that wasn't my name; it was the one given to me when they stole me from my home, from my family . . . I don't think I would recognize my real name if they told it to me, or the language it was spoken in.

I can't remember my language . . . my mother's voice, the warmth of her hug, especially not now while being encased in a dead, hollow tree in the cold fall months.

I heard them give up and walk away toward the residential school, leaving me, evidently not caring whether I lived or died.

I crawled from the tree, brushing my body free of mud and bugs, as much as I could at least, and as my heart slowed to a normal pace, I found myself chilled to the bone, and my teeth chattered no matter how quiet I tried to remain. I feared they'd return.

Slowly, I started making my way through the forest, remembering so vaguely the advice my grandfather gave me about living off the land, telling me to not fear nature as it was where we laid our home. But I couldn't help but fear. I could barely see my bruised and battered hands in front of my face. I could barely see the dangers before me through my tears; they were tears for all those I'd left behind in the school: my brother, who I had only seen once in those walls and never saw him again; my friend . . . who I left crying in her bed.

What had been done to us, what was being done to us, was horrifying . . . but so many others fell prey to their tales, believing it as normal. I couldn't . . . no, I wouldn't let my mind fall in line with their tricks because how easy it would be to do. I wouldn't look at my skin with disgust because I was taught differently . . . before they stole my mother's voice. I could hear her tell me I was beautiful, but they beat that from me . . . or at least they tried.

The darkness led me nowhere; I'd tripped over more stumps and twigs than I knew there to be in this place, scraping my knees and hands even more. The creaks of the branches and cracks of the twigs made me press against the trees in cover, fearing each sound was one of them approaching. Not dreading it was a bear or wolf, no, but instead, I feared it was one of the cruel beasts, the demons, I hear in my head—their pale skin and bright eyes more terrifying than this darkness ever could be.

As I stumbled deeper into the forest, farther away from the school, I realized I was lost. I knew this was likely from the moment I stepped foot in this forest, but that hadn't stopped me, nothing had until exhaustion finally took me over. I found a bed of grass, and I curled up and felt myself drift into a world of nightmares.

I was walking down the halls with my head down, my books pressed close to my chest, and I felt his hand on my shoulder. I looked up to see his pale, horrifying face looking down at me as he began leading me down the hall toward his office.

I would have screamed myself awake any other night, but, instead, tonight my mother came to my aid and pulled me away from that world and brought me to a brightly illuminated, sun-draped forest; her arms wrapped around me, holding me tight as she spoke to me in my language; it was a far-forgotten tongue, one stolen from me.

"My little fox," she said, smiling and hugging me so tight. The hug was so warm I could have mistaken it for the sun. Then she said, "I miss you. Are you going to come home to me?"

I looked back at her, and she was as beautiful as ever, even more so than I remembered. "They said you abandoned me . . . ," I said. My lip trembled as I saw the tears fill her eyes.

"Oh sweetheart, I would never. I fought for you as hard as I could. I held onto you as long as I was able, but . . . they won."

I shook from the cold, or maybe the sadness, I don't know, but she held me tighter, steadying me.

"Your brother is already here. He's waiting for you. We both are."

I looked up, and beside her was my brother, his toothless grin brighter than I had ever seen it before, and I wanted to go where they were, but before I could say a thing to my kin, he turned and ran off into the forest giggling, just how I remember he sounded.

I turned to my mother, and she let me go. As she stood to her feet, she gently said, "Come, my little fox, we don't have much time. We'll be waiting for you by morning."

I went to stand to my feet to follow her into the forest, watching as the sun went with her, leaving me in a cold, dimly lit, frozen place and time.

Come morning, I didn't wake up—not how I was supposed to anyway. By daybreak, the first snow of the year had fallen. It had come early, hiding all evidence of my escape—and of my doom.

I lay there now, frozen and enveloped in ice, never to be found, for no one is looking. Yet do not mourn me, do not pray for me, pray for the ones still held captive by the memories and the horrors because while I did not wake in my body, I awoke in another.

My body warm and filled with life and soul, I awoke as a kit in the warmth of my mother's den, my sibling and I pressed close to her. Our mother guided us out into the snow to play, to watch our happiness flourish, and to begin our life anew. Together.

Michelle Sylliboy photo

Joanne Arnott
Métis

Gathering Voices
On receiving submissions for 'Mothers Journey'

Beautiful ladies
spirits shine through words
on thin pages, laughter shakes me
grief glistens
adding lustre to my view
indignation
hot
rises within
what spills over
is love
love and conviction

Beautiful grandmother
the view from your porch
is just amazing
it has opened up my home
to the voices of a farflung choir
of articulating women
heartsongs rising from bush
and inner city
dancing like the sun across
the long grass
of this
wild prairie

Maisyn Sock
Mi'kmaq First Nation

A Daughter's Appreciation

Mother.
N'kij.
Mom.
Kloqo'wej
Starr.

This story is unlike any other. It's a story about a woman who had to continue, and about a woman who shines so brightly that her name suits her perfectly—Starr.

I was brought into this world with nothing but love. Love from my parents and love from the person I shared the womb with.

Starr is a warrior, one of her kind. She has fought many battles, some that only she knows.

This story is about how I realized my mother was more than just a warrior—she was a gift from god.

It all started one day when I was struggling the most in my life, but then I thought of everything I learned from, Ms. Starr Paul. My mom. As days went by and I thought life would hurt me more, I realized the strength that held me all together stemmed from her. A strong Indigenous woman. A single mother of seven. A leader. A voice for her language. A voice for her people.

I realized that life hurt me, and as I tried to make sense of it all, I know my mother thought of me every day and every night hoping one day I'd be back home to be nurtured and cared for. Her strength and her thinking of me continued to keep me going when all I thought of life was sadness and hopelessness.

I watched the days go by . . . and the nights . . . while Mom had to figure out how to fight back and how to continue to fight to have the life we do have now.

My mother is an educated woman, and she had to build the life and future she wanted. She had to fight. Fight for her education, fight for her voice—she fought with a purpose of knowing that everything she did was more than just for her—it was for her children and future children yet to come.

When racism found its way to my mother, there was no way she would stand down. She used all her power and her voice to be vocal about the change she wanted. She told that man, "You are discriminating against me!" She knew that wasn't the last time she'd see that man. My mother fought to get her voice heard, and she won. That man was educated, but after being so ignorant toward my mom, he learned a few things. He did not know what kind of storm was coming.

My mother gave us the best childhood she could. Whether it was road trips, trips to the movies, or reading books in different accents, my mom did the best she could, and I can see that now. I can see the struggles she endured and how she overcame them. I can see her shining.

My mother is the light that made me who I am.

My mother gave me and all my siblings gifts. Gifts she is unaware of. She gave each of us something so unique and different. She always tells us about how she does not know where we all get it from, but it's from her. It's her teachings that molded us into the individuals we have become.

One of the biggest teachings she ever taught me was that my words matter. What I say and how I say things will stick to each of the people I encounter on my path. What I say to someone that day could change them positively or negatively, and I now know that I have that power. My mother made me someone who is deeply reflective and made me think about what I say to other people. For that I am grateful because that made me into the person I am today.

My mother is a simple woman. She cares for her people and her family. She is very culturally oriented, and she loves community. My mother inspired me to volunteer in my community and to become more involved. She gave me the gift of helping others. Starr is the definition of determined.

I could go on and on about who my mother is, and what she has done to give me the life I have. But there are no words to thank her for the strength she instilled in my siblings and me, the endless reassurance she gives me, the spunk she inspires within me, and the pride she instills in me to be Mi'kmaw. She made me into the proud Mi'kmaw woman I am today.

Wela'lin, Mom, *wela'lin ujit msit kowey*. Thank you, Mom, thank you for everything.

Pixabay image

Edōsdi /Judith C. Thompson

Tahltan Band - Tahltan and Gitxsan descent

My Grandparents: Memory Keepers

When I think of my grandparents,
memories of my childhood flood my senses.
I can hear my Granny whistling like a bird as she worked in her kitchen.
I can smell the freshly baked bread,
taste the melting butter on that warm bread
– butter always tasted better at Granny's house!
I can picture their old oil stove,
the wringer washing machine.
The wonderful smell of Granny's soft cheek when I kissed her hello and
goodbye.

I can see Grandpa sitting on the edge of their bed,
listening to the Vancouver Canucks' hockey game on a transistor radio.
Sticks of wrapped Juicy Fruit gum tucked behind his ear
in anticipation of the arrival of his grandchildren,
kissing his cheek and him making a popping sound!
The sound of my grandfather's beloved country music fills the house
as do his stories about the different musicians.
Grandpa's pictures,
which he loved to bring out to share with family and guests,
especially ones of his mother, father,
and him as a handsome young man, are still vivid in my memory.

My relationship with my grandparents
up until the late 1980s
was one of grandchild/grandparents.
I always felt like a little girl around them,
even upon becoming an adult.
When I expressed my desire to learn more about our Tahltan language
and culture,
my grandparents embraced both me and my interest
and began to teach me the language, stories, traditions, and family history.

This was when our relationship deepened and elevated to a new level.
I now have new memories through their wonderful storytelling.
Images of my grandparents' life in Telegraph Creek.
I can picture Grandpa as an eight-year-old boy being summoned by Elders
to help beat soapberries by hand.
Of course, he had to scrub his whole arm before he was put to work!
My grandmother, who had her first child at eighteen (my mom),
waiting in anticipation for her children to come home from school
so she could wrestle and play with them.
My grandfather's stories of building the road into Telegraph Creek,
such as "Toad Hill."
My Granny's regret of not letting her mother
give her children Tahltan names when they were born.
Picturing Granny making rabbit snares out of willow branches as a
young girl.
Imagining her drying choke cherries
with her mother in the hot sun on an oil cloth
and then storing them in four-pound jam cans.

My grandmother once said to me,
"You have never been ashamed of your grandfather and me.
You love us for who we are."
Granny and Grandpa grew up during a time when being Tahltan,
being "Indian,"
was not something to be proud of.
Granny's father, of Irish and Dutch descent,
did not want his Tahltan wife to teach their children her language.
However, when he was away at work,
Tsahtsoymā, Agnes Vance (nee Quock),
would speak Tahltan to her children.
Grandpa's mother, Kitty Tatosa,
Istostē, died when he was only four years old.
Frank Callbreath, Grandpa's father,
of Scottish and Cherokee descent,
allowed his son to learn our language
from the Tahltan men who worked at his ranch.

Granny and Grandpa, considered to be
semi-fluent or silent speakers,
were able to help each other out
by remembering stories, phrases, words, or names.
After being married for almost seventy-eight years,
they were the "keepers" of each other's memories.
I am grateful that they have passed those memories to me,
mechā Edōsdi.

Edōsdi's grandparents ~ Monica Lamb-Yorski photo

John Williams
George Gordon First Nation

Well Water

I walked along the new gravel road, the rocks crunch-crunching beneath every step I had to take. The air was still and hot. The finest particles of dust remained suspended above the road from when the truck sped past me a while ago.

I had tried to get the truck to stop. I heard it coming up behind me on the road clear enough; what little muffler the truck had left did not stop the exploding BANG THUMP of the engine from reaching my ears long before I could see the rusty vehicle. I stepped carefully down into the ditch as the truck approached; I had to move careful because the left side of my belly felt like it was on fire. As the truck got closer, I waved my right arm slowly in the air. Just lifting my arm made the fire spread. I was so thirsty. I just wanted some water. The truck did not slow down. The driver honked his horn twice, and the girl in the passenger seat threw an empty can at me as they sped by.

I was so thirsty. My shirt and pants were wet with blood on the left side of my body, and the dust that the truck raised off the road stuck to my wet clothes. I struggled back up on to the road. I started walking again. I had to keep walking. I was so thirsty. The well water at my kookum's house was the best water in the world. That was where I was going. My kookum is my mother's mother.

This morning, I woke up really early. Earlier than my kookum but after my moshum. My moshum is my mother's father. Moshum let the screen door slam shut, which had woken me up. Moshum would have gone to the barn first thing and Kookum would be up in time to have breakfast and tea made for when he got back to the house. I lay in bed for maybe a minute when I saw the rifle. It was cradled in the gun rack on the closet door and there was a box of shells on the shelf below. I was not supposed to take anything more powerful than a BB gun out of the house when I was by myself, but . . .

I did not have time to get dressed. I grabbed up my clothes, the rifle and the box of shells, and hurried as silently as I could out the back door. I slowed down enough to put on my shoes and to make sure the door did not slam shut. I looked quickly down to the barn. The horses were just starting to gather around the big door. Any second that door would open and there would be Moshum, and I knew, I just knew, he would look right at me and I would be caught. I did not want to get caught. I crouched down as low as I could and ran into the bushes across the road, my jeans and red t-shirt waving behind me.

I ran through the bushes until I reached a path where I stopped to get dressed in my dusty jeans and t-shirt. I was just wondering what to do with the rifle and bullets when a rabbit scrambled out of the underbrush and in a flurry of dead leaves scurried down the path ahead of me. I knew what I was going to do today. I was going to hunt rabbits. But I had to get away from the house so nobody would hear the rifle. I was eleven; I should be hunting rabbits to feed my family, not doing what I did yesterday when I got caught playing in the hay bales and had to go pick berries with the girls and little boys. If I came home with a rabbit for dinner, no one would care that I took the rifle.

With the thought of showing everyone how grown-up I was, my plan started to change. I went from getting one rabbit to bringing home two, no three, of the biggest rabbits you ever saw. They would be so big I would have trouble carrying those four rabbits home. But first I had to get away from the house.

I rushed down the trail until it reached the old horse path that paralleled the new gravel road. There was a thick hedgerow between the two roads, so no one would see me if they happened to drive by. I kept my pace fast and passed a couple of old homesteads. I knew these to be the old houses of my ancestors. Foundations of homes from people long past, now heavily overgrown. I came to the place where the hedgerow gradually disappeared and the horse path melted into the new gravel. There was a wide, lightly grown-in path that veered to the left. I went to the left.

Going down this path, I imagined how many people I would feed with my five world-record-setting rabbits. All my cousins and aunts and uncles would be at the house for dinner. My moshum would teach me how to skin and dress a rabbit, and I would do it perfectly on my fifth try. I would present the carcasses to Kookum, who would butcher them up and make two large stockpots of stew. Once the butchered rabbits were simmering, Kookum would add in fresh snap peas from the vines that grew around her house, carrots two days out of the garden, yellow potatoes dug this year, and some things I could not recognize that she had gone out and collected herself. There would be fresh-made, still-warm blueberry and Saskatoon berry bannock dripping with melted butter to dip into the stew. The smell would be strong and inviting throughout, and outside of, her home.

I came to a clearing with an old car slowly rusting and dead lying right in the centre of all the trees. The tires had been burned away. The paint was bleached and fire-stained to a pale blue; all the glass had long since been smashed out. But it wasn't an old abandoned car, it was a tank, just like Grampa, my dad's father, had described in his stories from the War.

I dropped to one knee. I was a soldier like Grampa in World War II. That wicked German tank was keeping my entire platoon pinned down. I was the only one who could save us. I fumbled with the box of bullets and spilled a bunch onto the ground. My shaking hands finally managed to load a bullet into the rifle. My rifle loaded and ready for action, I charged at the tank screaming at the top of my eleven-year-old lungs. Grampa always said, "You gotta get on top and shoot into the tank if you want to get the Germans." I raced at the tank. I stepped onto the chrome bumper of the old car with one foot. Then with my other foot, I jumped off the hood and onto the roof. I aimed my rifle downward as I landed on top of the old car. The rusted metal could not resist the weight of me jumping onto it. The top of the old car collapsed. At the very first buckling of the roof, my body tensed up and I mindlessly pulled the trigger on the rifle.

CRACK!

The roof collapsing had thrown me off balance, and I fell back onto the hood and then bounced down to the ground on the driver's side. Everywhere above my knees hurt. I could not breathe. My hands instinctively grabbed for the source of pain, and I screamed.

I think I must have fallen asleep, because the next thing I remember, I was running down the path screaming for help, my left hand holding onto my side where I had a burning pain. I did not run far. I could not breathe very well, and I got tired fast. Soon I was just plodding through the dense forest, putting one foot in front of the other. Sweat started out all over my body. I looked down at my left side, thinking I would see flames where I was holding myself. There was blood all over my hand and a big wet stain on my t-shirt. I was so thirsty.

I reached the intersection of the horse path and gravel road. I knew no one would see me on the horse path, so I started walking down the road. A truck came toward me. I was on fire, and I was so thirsty. I tried to get the truck to stop. I waved, and the truck honked and someone threw a can out the passenger window at me as they sped by. The truck's dust hung in the still and hot air.

I knew two things. The crunch-crunching of the gravel road under every step I had to take and I was going to Kookum's house. She had the best well water in the world.

Art by
Jerry
Smaaslet

Shauntelle Dick-Charleson
Hesquiaht and Songhees

Card

I am not a mathematician
I am not a math teacher
But I know a thing or two about numbers

Shauntelle D'lyla Dick-Charleson is an Indian within the meaning of
The Indian Act's 27 statutes of Canada 1985

I am defined as a number

I am defined as "Indian" because of a card
I carry in my wallet
But why?
Why am I called an Indian
When I was born 22 hours 30 minutes and 2000 kilometers away
From India?
So why the hell are you calling me Indian?

Why am I just a number?

Why am I looked down upon as "second class"?
Is it because of my skin colour?

Why am I anything less than what I am?

I am not Indian; I don't mean any disrespect
They are a native of their land
And I'm a native of mine

My name is NOT 661001702
It is TICEN and HUUPQUESTAHH

I am from Songhees and Hesquiaht
NOT INDIA
You probably didn't know that I have a card

Every 2-3 years, I have to re-new my card to prove my identity
I have to pay $15
To get a new card, I have to travel from Victoria to Port Alberni
Lekumgen to Tsehat
This equals
5 hours and 29 minutes and 191 kilometres

I am not just a bag of meat you get at the store
I don't have an expiry date 00/00/0000
I don't have a barcode IIIIOOOOIIO OIIIIIO

I cannot be defined as just a card, as just a number
I feel
I breathe

So why do I have to carry a card
To say that I'm Native
When it's in my blood?

I shouldn't be told that "you don't have a status card,
so you're not Native"

I doubt the girl next to me has to carry one to say that she's from
Russia, Germany, Italy, China, or Australia
While I'm from here—MY NATIVE LAND
Proving my identity

So why do I
Have to be defined as a number?
I am a human being just like everyone else

If one race is going to have a card then all of us should have one
And if you don't want a card then I shouldn't need one

My name is not 661001702
My gifted name is
TICEN and HUUPQUESTAHH
But you can call me

Shauntelle

Jo Chrona
Ts'msyen, member of the Kitsumkalum Band

between the borders

"you should float between the borders," she says . . .
"i do," i respond

i exist between the borders . . .
have dwelt there, and here,
a lifetime, or two, it seems

between the borders that define sexuality
between the borders that define culture
between the borders that define identity

between the borders of your skin and mine,
between this living in, and out, of my mind
boundaries defined, and blurred
celebration . . . and denial
patience . . . and haste
harmony . . . and discordance

between the boundaries that define
self and other
in the spaces
between our words,
where we make meaning . . .
in the places
between our bodies
where we yearn to connect . . .
in the energy
between our spirits
where we seek to know . . .

"i do," i say again

Spencer Sheehan-Kalina
Métis Community of Maniwaki

At Home

Days spent digging up dandelion roots,
culling blackberry bushes that have colonized my garden;

pulling trash from the earth,

beer bottle caps, cigarette butts, shreds of plastic bags;
For the reward of a neglected patch of garden:
the red hips of a scraggly rose bush,

tender, nourishing, ripe enough to eat.

~

If you make it with enough love,
this recipe is the taste of bliss,

Grandmother instructs,

these days you need to know how to cook
for yourself, for nourishment and joy,

rosehips and sugar mix into boiling water

if you're careful to preserve it right
you'll have it for years to come,

she pours the mix into mason jars, seals them,

in the good times and in the bad times;
It's the preservation that's most important.

I'm now trying to do as she taught me, years ago.

Anytime is a good time for the happiness of sweet jam,
for the happiness of sweet love at home.

~

Morning birdsong, grassy jazz of limbs caressing
bed sheets, the scent of rosehip jam spread on toast.

Nothing is as it used to be,

Grandmother often used to say.
Every day passing, this becomes truer than when she'd said it last.

My grandmother is gone, I've my own home now,
I make my own rosehip jam to spread on my own toast,

but the past does not abandon us, *Nothing is as it used to be,*
but what used to be is still here, even if only in eroding memories,
like in a simple recipe that Grandmother and I used to make at home.

*Art by
Spencer
Sheehan-
Kalina*

Jeremy Ratt
Métis, Peter Ballantyne Cree Nation

The Aboriginal Identity

Being raised in alienation of your own culture is a very strange experience, to say the least, and the coming together of many individuals to celebrate their culture's history was something I could never feel truly ingrained with. There was a sense of identity dissociation throughout my childhood, where I found myself in a position that belonged to neither side, but somewhere in the middle. And with more and more birthday candles being placed on the cake, I developed an askew perspective of my own people and the people around my people.

In my years of watching the world unfold, I have found one thing to be entirely true. The development and understanding of diverse groups has been growing exponentially. Ethnic communities, LGBTQ+ communities, and various religious beliefs have new foundations of respect and inclusion within our everyday world. This understanding still leaves humanity with a lot of work to do, but we as a society have begun to contextualize our mistakes, learn from them, and use them as a stepping stone toward a brighter and better world. However, as said, the construction of that idea comes with the deconstruction of previous misconceptions. One example of this revolves around Canada's Aboriginal and Métis background. As a member of the Métis community, I have witnessed an ongoing division of opinions when it applies to the image of First Nations people from the eyes of non-Native people. This observation came from my very own upbringing.

I was born in Saskatoon, Saskatchewan. My parents were of differentiating backgrounds, with my father being of French descent, while my mother was of full Aboriginal blood, hailing from northern Saskatchewan's Peter Ballantyne Cree Nation. Because of this, I was born in a fifty/fifty split of two vastly different cultures. In my infancy, my father left my family, long before I could even start remembering anything. This left my young and struggling mother alone to raise me.

Thus, a stark contrast arose. In my childhood, I had the pale skin of a white boy, but I was raised in a primarily Aboriginal setting. So more often than not, I was an outlier.

Alongside my mother, I moved from town to town. I went from Saskatoon to Prince Albert, Prince Albert to Regina, Regina to Invermere, and finally Invermere to Kelowna, BC. And with each new school and new background, the alienation of my own culture became more cemented. I looked pale and white, and because of this, I spent a majority of my life viewing myself as a white child. It only made sense in my very young thinking at the time. As for my view on Aboriginal culture, I saw two different versions of a story. Through my mother, I learned the importance of togetherness in a Native family, the importance of helping one another, helping yourself, and being thankful to live another day on this earth.

However, through the screen of a television, that type of emotional connection and understanding of Aboriginal culture was muted. As a child, I saw cowboys and Indians fighting each other, with the Indians depicted as the "losers" a majority of the time. And from then on, my young eyes started to see this image everywhere. Whether it be kids playing in the park or hearing people on the news, it felt like Native was a dirty word. It made me feel strange about embracing my own roots and background, knowing that I didn't inherently look Native, and that it was seemingly better to get by in the world posing as a white man.

These feelings finally subsided when I moved to Kelowna in February of 2014. I was approaching adolescence, and from my journey, I had an angry heart and an introverted personality. I didn't know what to do with myself, and I certainly didn't know how I was going to contribute to the outside world. I had trouble making friends when I first moved into town, so I spent a majority of my time at my school's Gathering Room, a place where Aboriginal kids could seek out assistance and safety. There, the Aboriginal advocates spent time getting to know me, and they eventually nurtured my skills and talents. From then on, this encouragement built a foundation for who I was and who I wanted to be. I discovered my passion for writing, which would then stem into public speaking, and then grow into the fields of acting and broadcasting. By the end of the year, the difference was night and day.

Looking back on it now, I came to terms with my Aboriginal roots without even realizing it. In finding my own identity and learning to love myself, I made peace with my origin. The feelings of alienation and confusion have all but faded. As of this moment, I currently seek to use my passions for acting and writing to give back to my Native roots and tear down the false images of Indians—images that had stopped me from embracing my diversity. The key to equality and mutual respect between cultures does not come from a restructuring of formalities, but instead it arrives from the restructuring of relationships. As an Aboriginal and a Canadian, I can only hope we develop a better foundation for future Aboriginal and Non-Aboriginal people to work together and create an improved level of understanding.

Art by Phil Joe

Dennis Saddleman
Nlaka'pamux Nation, Coldwater Band

Web of Life

Beautiful woman
Beautiful woman, you are young, going towards eighteen
You are woman and wife
Wife of a hard-working man
Hard-drinking man
You have a daughter
Your daughter went to bed with an empty stomach
You sat in the kitchen
Sat in the chair
You waited for your sweetie
The one they call tall, dark, and handsome
The one who went to work at the saw mill
It's your sweetie's payday
You wondered where he is
He hasn't come home yet
You thought he might be at the bar with the boys
You were worried that your sweetie will spend all the money on booze
You were worried there was no food in the cupboards
And you wondered if there will be enough money for the bills
You looked at the clock, My gawd! It's almost midnight!
You sprang from the chair
You paced back and forth
You went this way and that way
You went in a frenzy
You loved your sweetie very much
You were afraid he might end up in jail or the hospital
You lit a cigarette, took a deep drag
Took another deep drag, hoping it would calm your nerves
You went to the window to find any signs of your sweetie, there were
none

Angry words came silently
You wanted to shout, but you were afraid to wake up your daughter
Angry words raced through your mind
You wanted to strangle your sweetie for making you worry
You wished your sweetie didn't drink
You wished there was no booze in this world
You went to your daughter's room, to see if she was sleeping
Yes she was sleeping, she was probably dreaming of a hot meal
You stared at your daughter, you watched her sleep
You kissed your daughter's forehead
Suddenly! You heard the family dog bark outside
For a moment, happiness emerged inside of you
Happiness danced in your thoughts
My sweetie! My sweetie! He's home! He's home!
You rushed to greet your sweetie
You heard footsteps on the other side of the door
You watched the door knob, it turned, the door opened
You held your breath, your heart sank
Your happiness shattered like glass
Your sweetie staggered in. He reeked with alcohol
He didn't say hello. Instead, he demanded your body
You protested with fear. Protesting made your man angry
He backhanded you, your upper lip split
He grabbed you, his fingers like vise grips
He threw you across the room, you slammed hard against the wall
The wall shook, the night didn't want to be night
The river near your home, it flowed away
The wolves, the wolves in the hills, they howled mournfully
A spider! A spider on the ceiling, it watched you fall to the floor
The spider with many eyes, the only witness to your physical abuse
The spider came down, came down on a silver string
The spider built a web
Built a web of life just for you

Jillian Wicks
Alexander First Nation

Sorrow Indian

I grew up sheltered and protected
I became trusting and caring
Everyone all around guarding my world
I did not see what others did
Cultivating a flourishing, nurturing soul
Fearful of the outside pain that would taint it
They told me to go to school, to learn "the ways", without saying it
Finally, the day came
My fellow peers excelled and prospered
Attending college and university
I was followed my first day, and most days
But I kept on, in denial as to why
So I left that path; it became too unsafe
When I was asked why? It's free for you!
Looking into eyes that will never know the feeling, I simply say it
wasn't what I wanted anymore
I turn my cheek to the truth
I feel dishonest with myself, but have done nothing wrong
It's not fair . . .

Life goes on, I hold my first born, looking into his light eyes and at his
fair skin
I feel relieved, he will not be obvious
It will be *fair* for him
I no longer have just me and begin my journey of motherhood and
the sacrifices along with it
As each simple daily routine changes, it seems no big deal
Until, all alone, I am exhausted and wonder deep into my mind why I
really have certain habits
Must look clean and proper every day
Mommy doesn't get to have easy days with messy buns and sweat pants
Can't be mistaken as *another one* on welfare

My husband sees I'm exhausted, says buy yourself some new things,
make time for *you*
I'm happy he sees that
Off I go with my baby in tow
Quickly things go off course
Mommy gets followed in every store and deep stares into my stroller,
not at the baby, but for "items"
I remember I do not look my best
Turning my cheek to the truth
I leave the mall
I scramble to dig my car keys out of the diaper bag
An older couple walks by staring and whispering
My baby begins to fuss
We're settled in the car
And I hear I knock on my window
Mall security
I roll my window down
"Hello ma'am, you heading out?"
Yes
I look blankly at him, wondering if I have done anything wrong
"Is that *your* Baby in the back?"
Fuck you
But, I smile and nod my head yes
Worried to show any hostility that may give into the stereotype
I feel like a disgraceful mother for not flying off the handle to protect
my cub, my world
It just isn't *fair*
I've done nothing wrong . . .

Life goes on a bit more
My little tribe has grown by two
My skin is thicker, and I've become introverted
Protecting my world, my cubs
They do not know *what* they are
I see missing Indigenous women posts plastered everywhere
Could that have been me? Perhaps that almost was me?
Will that be me?

Will it be my daughter?
Will it be my sister?
I see reconciliation articles and clips every day
I see why I was so sheltered and protected
My son looks at me with his big blue eyes and asks when will he be
brown like his *moshum* and me
I tell him he has the most beautiful heart and to *never* let that change

I feel guilty for "contributing" to assimilation
I did not commit it knowingly
I hear and feel the cries of my ancestors
inside my heart . . . like I was just born with it already there
It's not fair, I have done nothing wrong
I thought I was fighting it, I thought I was proud
And here I am . . .

I am *another* sorrow Indian . . .

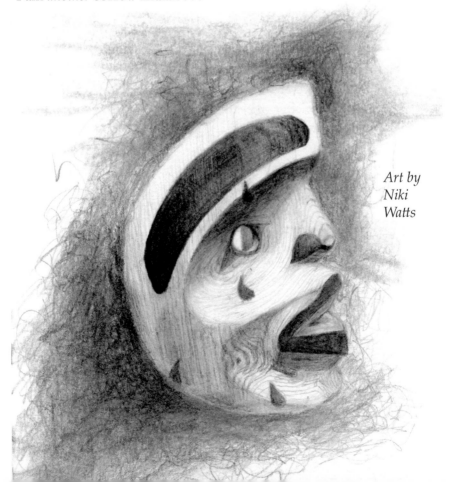

Art by
Niki
Watts

Visions and Visitations

Authored by the ILRP 100 (Indigenous Learning and Recognition Portfolio) class at Vancouver Island University. *Transcribed and woven together by class members: Keandra Thomas, Quinn James, Hayden Taylor, Joanna Harris, and Francis Guerrero*

"Breakfast!" shouted Mom, hurrying downstairs. Mike, still in bed, knew he'd be the last one there. His little sister was probably already at the table. She's always first—ready and excited for school. Grandma, always up at sunrise, doesn't waste time; she dished out breakfast as Mom entered the kitchen in her frantic-morning mood, which seemed even more panicked today. Dad readied his resumes on a side table before sitting down for breakfast. Mike sauntered in last and sat down. Grandma cleared her throat to get everyone's attention for morning prayer. As everyone closed their eyes, Mike reached for a piece of toast and started eating. Grandma didn't let this interrupt her prayer, though Mom shot Mike an angry glare. Prayer ends with Grandma asking for the Creator's help when Family Services comes to visit tonight. Mike yawned and stood up. Breakfast consisted of an egg and a piece of toast, which took Mike all of a minute to eat. Dad passed half of his toast to Grandma. Grandma, as always, gave the extra food to sister. Mike shook his head; sister always got the extras.

"Why is Family Services coming?" asked sister.

Mom and Dad stopped in place.

"They're worried we're not providing you with everything you need," replied Father.

Mom added, "They'll be here at 6:30 tonight, so please be home early to make sure the house is spotless."

"Screw that," responded Mike, "I'm not doing that!"

"Mike—," pleaded Mom, but he was out the door, storming toward his car.

"He's young," said Grandma.

"Why is he always so mad?" asked sister.

Grandma replied, "He has much to learn."

Driving away from the house, Mike looked back to see Grandma walking sister to school just like Grandpa used to do with him. Sister was always telling Mike the new words and songs Grandma had taught her.

Mike didn't go to school, instead he hung around with a couple of his buddies. Nothing had gone Mike's way today. He only had 200 bucks until next payday, and looking down at his gas gauge, he saw he was near empty; plus, he was frustrated that Family Services was going to check in on his family again. Mike's mind wasn't focused on the road, and he was driving over the speed limit. Coming around a bend, Mike thought he saw a raven on the road and swerved out of the way. He lost control of his car and piled into a telephone pole. Mike's head hit the steering wheel; his vision blurred, and just before he lost consciousness, he swore that raven hopped up on the crushed-in hood of his car and stared at him.

In the darkness, the sound of fast-paced flapping could be heard, coming from the west. A loud call came from the sky above, "*Kwa! Kwa!*" It was a young raven, grasping a glowing sphere in its mouth; the realm began to brighten. Raven then dove by Mike, gently setting down the glowing sphere—the source of the light. The realm brightened. Though, shadows remained at the edges.

"You lost?" asked Raven.

Mike was surprised by the Raven's ability to talk.

"I'm a messenger. I carry messages far and wide, especially if an Elder gives me one. I have a message for you!"

The raven reminded Mike of someone, with its energy and chattiness.

"Well, what's the message?" asked Mike.

"You've been listening to the wrong messages!"

"Talk is cheap! I'll listen to whatever and whoever I want."

"Actually, talk is free," replied Raven. "But you can miss out on much knowledge if you don't listen. Also, what you pass on can have great effects on the world around you."

"What are you going on about?"

"Your people have a powerful oral tradition, but if nobody listens, this knowledge will be lost forever."

"Why are you telling me this? You know nothing about me!"

"Remember when Grandpa walked you to school? Remember how he'd try and talk about his days growing up in the old village and the ways of his people? You told him not to walk with you, that you didn't want to hear those stories."

Mike was silent.

"That was just before he passed. Do you remember?"

Mike nodded.

"Would you change that moment if you could?"

"How was I to know he was going to die?"

"We are only here for a short time. We need to make time to listen and to respect our Elders. We need to listen to the right messages and learn of our traditions."

Memories of his grandpa came flooding back. They were difficult for Mike to swallow.

"Anyways. I'll just leave the sun here to brighten up your day. I have messages to deliver after all. Gotta go! *Kwa!*"

Raven took flight and was gone as fast as she arrived, fading into the distance.

From the north, a flush of snow fell and Mike noticed a wolf running toward him. The wolf approached, and as had Raven, Wolf spoke to him. "Do you understand why I am here?"

"No. I don't even know where 'here' is."

Wolf explained that Mike was here because he has the wrong perspective.

Mike, confused, asked, "So, is this another lesson then?"

Wolf replied, "Indeed. But here you cannot run away as you have been doing."

"I don't run from anything."

"Mike, you try to go it alone when things get tough instead of sticking around and helping your pack. Do you help your family? Do you support them?"

"Well, I've just been focusing on other things lately."

"Family is irreplaceable. I know my pack is the only thing I can always count on," said Wolf.

"Do you know anything about how family works? Do you know what it's like having random people show up to your house asking questions, having your sister be the favourite?"

Wolf replied, "I know what it's like to work as a pack to defend one's territory and ways of living, yes."

"My buddies and I are tight—they're my family."

"They won't fight for you like your pack will, Mike. To step up and to help care for your family is a tough role. Soon you'll realize family is treasure and more important than anything because they won't leave you through your rough patches. You have to learn how to protect them regardless of the situation."

"They make me so angry," replied Mike.

"I didn't say it would be easy," said Wolf. "There will be tough times. But even then, I support my pack; I protect them. If I don't bring back food or protect them from others, they suffer, and then I suffer too in seeing their pain. I look out for my old ones and for my young, for they are most at risk. Your family suffers, and you have the power to change that."

"I can't fix everything!" Mike shouted.

"We do only what we can, and we pray that it is enough," said Wolf, turning north into the falling snow and back to his pack.

From the east came a buffalo, breaking off from the herd and making its way toward Mike. The lone buffalo stood tall in a plain of long sweet grass. The rest of the herd ran toward the clouds in the distance, rumbling the earth as they did so. Buffalo, now close, stared at Mike with familiar eyes. Buffalo began with a serenity prayer. Following the prayer, Buffalo asked, "Do you know why it is important to open with prayer?"

Mike had no clue as he usually ate or didn't pay attention to prayers.

"I say the Serenity Prayer to provide me with the power to accept the things that I cannot change, and it reminds me to have courage to make the changes I can."

"They're just words."

"I have lived through awful times and have seen the suffering of my herds as we were all but wiped out. If I let my fear, my grief, or my anger control me, I would be of no use to those who need me. While I carry this pain within me, I try to move forward in a good way. These words help me remember that."

"How is this supposed to help me?"

"Your temper controls you. Why is this?"

Mike answered, "I . . ."

Buffalo continued, "Your parents lost their culture when they were young; it was torn from them, but they had the courage to make a change; they include a prayer every morning, they brought your grandparents to live with you, and they want to make sure the house is ready for the visit."

Mike was tired of being angry all of the time, and he hadn't made an effort to change this. He suddenly felt heavy and tired.

"Mike, happiness is a choice; you can choose to be happy and appreciative of what you've got rather than focusing on what you don't have. It's a choice that can be reinforced with prayer."

He hesitated a long moment before whispering, "Alright."

This smallest of acknowledgements released a weight from him. He wasn't happy in that moment, but he suddenly felt he had the potential to be, and he hadn't had that before.

Buffalo re-joined her herd, and Mike instantly missed her.

From the south, the wind started swirling. Mike looked for the source. High in the sky, an eagle starting its approach. Mike knew the eagle, now landing beside him, was here to help him on his journey.

"You too have a lesson for me, Eagle?" asked Mike.

Eagle gently replied, "I am here to share wisdom and the importance of traditional knowledge with you."

Eagle, like Buffalo, explained that if Mike were to continue living his ways, it would not serve him or his family well.

"Our people have been through many obstacles. Your parents and your grandparents are all survivors of trauma, and they, to this day, deal with their anger and hate," said Eagle.

Mike was confused. He hadn't noticed this before.

Eagle continued, "They are dealing with this in a healthy way, but you place your anger onto your family members, disrespecting them."

"Buffalo spoke of this," answered Mike.

"But what you might not know," said Eagle, "Is that when you were very young, your family had even less than they do now. Some of your anger stems from the privileges you think your sister gets. In those tough earlier times, you never went without food, even when they did. And they regularly went without."

Mike was speechless, unaware of the sacrifices his parents had made for him back then.

Eagle stretched her wings and said, "I tell you this so you realize the people before you have sacrificed much. You cannot let those sacrifices go unacknowledged. Learn of your peoples' past, learn of your traditions, and learn what it means to live in a good way."

Eagle leapt into the air and several wing beats later, she was gone.

Mike thought about how each of these teachings were connected. With this clarity, Raven's sphere rose and made its way to the centre of his vision. As it got closer, things got brighter and brighter; in each direction, all four spirit animals stood proud. Looking at them, he realized they reminded him of his family. At that moment, Mike woke up; getting out of his car, he looked over the wreckage. He was happy to be alive. He smiled and thought back to his visions.

Later that afternoon, Mike arrived home with arms filled with bags of groceries. The family all ran outside, confused as to why Mike was walking.

"Where is your car?" asked sister.

"That thing? I sold it for scrap. Bus is way more reliable," said Mike.

They all looked at him wide-eyed for a moment.

"Anyway, let's get these groceries inside—they're getting heavy! Plus, we've got to get ready for that visit. But first, dinner is on me.

*Included here are the names of all the students who made contributions to this piece: Quinn James, Hayden Taylor, Keandra Thomas, Joanna Harris, Francis Guerrero, Thomas Coon, Jackie Roper, Jade-Lynn Jensen, Natasha Frank, William Alger, Damion Charles, and Troy Good.
Edited by ILRP 100 instructor, Michael Calvert.

Connie Fife
Cree

Prayers

there are prayers to be said
uttered amongst winter winds
that bend tree or snap the heart
prayers to be sung in the dim light
of a northern Canadian sunset
prayers which bring crow to again
perch on shoulder
those to be placed in the cold
waters of glacier stream
to pull through
storm into skin
to praise forthcoming turbulence
caused by the movement of buffalo
hoof thundering across frozen ground
their scent left behind

*Art by
Leanna
Raven
Paul*

Maisyn Sock
Mi'kmaq First Nation

The Attempted Assassination on My Spirit

What do you see when you look at me?
What preconceived idea do you have of me?
Am I going to steal from you?
Am I only living off the government?
You think you see so many things, but
what you don't see is that I am
five times more likely to go missing or be murdered.
A stamped statistic on my young Mi'kmaw soul.

They tried so hard to get rid of the "Indian" problem, but
we weren't a problem at all.
Just different from them.
This country was built on racism, privilege, destruction, and lies.
All of these are alive and well in our "O Canada", but
we're too nice of a country to ever admit that.
Ignorance and uneducated people are the root of the problem.
Let's not forget the land this country was built on!
Because "Our home and Native land", eh?

After hundreds and hundreds of years of hardship,
How dare you look at me like that?
How dare you assume my path in life?
Trauma is embedded into my spirit.
Intergenerational trauma.
How can we as Indigenous people let that define us when
there's much more than that?

There is hope.
There is culture.
There is a sense of identity.
There is resilience.
There is help, there is community.

How can we look in the mirror and not be proud of who we are when the blood of our ancestors runs through our veins?
We are the truth, we are the rebirth.
We are L'nuk.

Michelle Sylliboy photo

Joe Starr
Haisla Nation

The Storm

The rain and wind paid another visit to the Heiltsuk, but this time there was something different. It was like they both had a message to deliver. There was something about the rain and wind that did not feel right to Wethl and the other ancient spirits. Wethl was the youngest of the ancient spirits, but he was considered by the others as an old soul. The other human spirits were confused by it all and did not understand why they were travelling on the ocean floor rather than on the land that they were accustomed to.

As they neared Go kwa aitow, one of the harvesting grounds, the spirits began to cry like the humans in physical form when they heard their old *gwa ya yu*, their mourning songs. Wethl spoke with the spirits, saying that he was given a message from the whale spirits that they were to gather at the underwater cave where the whales took refuge when something big happened in or on the ocean. What did the whale spirits know that the other spirits were unaware of? As the human spirits entered in the underwater cave, they noticed the smooth, dark walls, which were contrasted by the bold ochre-red images of blackfish and a humpback whale they knew lived in the ocean. One large image was of a blackfish with two dorsal fins and another with three dorsal fins. On the opposite wall was another blackfish with two heads facing one another with the mouths opening as if waiting to hunt for its next meal. On the ceiling of the cave was a massive humpback whale that had two wolves for its tail flukes. The floor of the cave had the image of the vertebrates of the different whales neatly interlocked like a tessellation. The interlocked vertebrates were protected with a clear film that looked like a huge jellyfish.

Now that the human and whale spirits were gathered inside the cave, a feeling suddenly overpowered them as if they were held captive and unable to leave. The human spirits leaned up against the cave walls as the *Heymas*, the Chief, of the whale spirits began his welcome. He then told them something was not right with what was happening with the humans. The spirits knew that the ocean has been sick for some time, but what could they do as spirits? Not too long ago, a huge boat, nothing like the canoes that were gentle with the ocean, ran aground, and this thick black substance escaped into the ocean. The black liquid was like octopus ink, and it made its way to the rocky beach, suffocating all of the life forms it came into contact with. The spirits were here again to witness the same event, but on a smaller scale. It was a much smaller boat that was towing a large box. The humans in this boat hit the rocks.

This confused the whale spirits again because the humans who live on the land and ocean along the coast know about the bashful rocks that prefer to hide below the surface of the choppy waters. The whales knew of the rocks and so did the humans. The humans who live in this area respected the bashful rocks and gave them names. The rocks are there to remind both the ocean and human animals to pay attention when travelling, whether it be during day or night.

The whale spirit *Heymas* reminded all of the spirits gathered in the cave about another big boat that recently ran aground during the night. The boat was carrying a lot of people and their strange boats that had wheels and could not travel on the water. There are still two humans in physical form inside that sunken boat.

To lighten the topic, the whale and human spirits reminisced about the time when they were both able to transition into each other's physical form; it was so long ago that neither of the spirits remembered when the humans forgot how to do this. The animals could still transition into human form, and the humans no longer notice even when it happens right in front of them.

Just as Wethl was about to speak, the human spirits noticed that the floor of the cave looked as if it was leaking something black. The whale spirits also saw this, but what could they say or do? It was a reminder of what the humans were responsible for. There were many things that the spirits no longer understood nor could they make any sense of.

Why was there so much rain? Rain that did not feel like rain. There was such a heaviness; it felt as if the rain too was in mourning because of the humans' carelessness once again. Even though the spirits were inside the cave, they could feel the intense downpour. The last time they felt this was when it rained frogs. It was the time when humans began to settle and call the coast home. The humans have old stories that tell of this event.

There was a black cloud that was doing an agitated dance on the surface of the water. The spirits did not recall ever experiencing this before, at least not the human spirits. This was their first time inside the ocean world. The humans and whales sensed that something was not right.

Before Wethl began to speak, all of the spirits present began to sing their old *gwa ya yu* in unison. The human spirits were at a loss about what to do. They have never had to comfort the animal spirits, those on the land and the water. Wethl was lost in thought, wondering why the whale spirits invited them to gather. The only thing Wethl could think of was that he knew the humans had evolved from the whales, way back in time. Wethl heard some of these stories, but the humans no longer know of these stories. This is old knowledge that Wethl sometimes wondered if the human spirits have given much thought to. It is as if nothing was making sense and logic had just vanished.

The human spirits are here to mourn with the whales. All were present to mourn the death of the important kelp beds, clam beds, barnacles, sea urchins, sea cucumbers, and other sea life which the human spirits had never thought of before. Did this mean that the human spirits, like the humans in physical form, were forgetting the ancient teachings? With all that has happened, is this the beginning of the fate of the people on the coast? The people whose way of life will now be altered.

What will the humans do now that the clams, sea urchins, salmon and the precious kelp have been affected? The kelp chose Go kwa aitow for their habitat, and the kelp harvested from here is ideal for the herring to lay their eggs on in the spring. Both men and women harvest the kelp just prior to the herring being ready to spawn. The humans remember one of the old teachings, and they pay close attention to the moon as she begins to tilt forward as if preparing to release the herring from her embrace. Even the spirits are able to feel the anticipation of the humans as the time neared for the herring to do what they have always done. The kelps are anchored in place with a length of string and a small rock. Each kelp was individually secured to a long rope. The old teachings said that the humans need to remain still and quiet while on the water during this important time for spawning. This is something the people have always done as far back as they can remember. Over time, the newer generations of humans either do not know of the old teachings, or they don't believe in what they call 'superstitions'. The humans heard the old chiefs attempt to pass this old knowledge, and they seemed to do the opposite. With the bigger boats and bigger motors, it was like the humans had to prove that they could spook the herring.

Fortunately, the humans still have the hemlock trees, the *ya ga* and *sya ahm*, which the old teachings told the people that the herring like to spawn on as well. This too is a treat for the people when the time arrives to harvest the herring eggs. It has only been in recent times that the people harvested the eggs on the flat kelp and sold them to people on the other side of the world to people who also rely on the ocean for their food. It is this demand that will devastate the people who rely on harvesting the kelp.

Wethl began to tell of what he saw before the big boats began travelling the coastal waters. There was a time when the Haisla would be loaded into their canoes and towed, by what they call a tug boat, to one of the salmon canneries in Owekeno territory. There was always a stop in Waglisla. The Haisla would visit for a few days while delivering the gifts of the precious oolichan oil, and dried oolichans, which were strung on long lengths of cedar bark. Both nations looked forward to this time of the year. After a brief visit, the Haisla returned to their canoes and continued on their journey to the cannery to which they were employed. The men seined for the salmon while the women salted and canned the salmon. The finished product was sold by the cannery owners to another part of the world. The salmon was sold to people who did not have the abundance of salmon the people had on the coast. The *gwe* loot did not make much money; it was the cannery owner who made the money. That was just the way things were.

By late fall when the salmon season came to an end, the Haisla began their journey back home, with a stop at Waglisla to continue their visit. When it was time to continue on their journey home, they would leave with gifts of dried and salted herring eggs, tin containers tightly packed with chopped seaweed, and thick cakes of dried seaweed. This is how the Haisla and the Waglisla maintained their connection. Over the years, this happened less and less. The Elders miss this, but with the new generations unwilling to continue this practice, what could they do?

Art by Niki Watts

What will become of the younger generation who may have only heard of the word *wa wa nu da*, or trading for food harvested from the water, and not actually participated in this important tradition? The human spirits see that the younger generation no longer eat the traditional food on a daily basis, nor do they help with the harvesting and preparing of the traditional foods. Change is happening quickly, and the spirits wondered if the humans are aware of the how the angry, unsettled weather, the spills of the black substance, and the loss of traditional ways are impacting how their way of life is evolving.

And now that the kelp beds may be destroyed for the herring to spawn on, what will it mean when the moon tilts over to release the herring?

Will the humans continue to ignore this important message?

Charla Lewis
Coast Salish, Squamish

INDIAN ACT

Hear, hear! I declare,
We must teach the Indian how to Act!
We must take their voice
And bind their mind,
Remove their choice
So they are blind.
Yes, yes, teach the Indian how to Act!
We must cut their hair
And scrub them clean,
Make them swear
Fealty to our Queen.
Quickly, quickly, before they can react,
We will teach the Indian how to Act!
For us to thrive
We must take control,
We must contrive
To break their soul.
This is our plight and our holy task,
To teach the Indian how to Act!
We must steal their young,
End family ties,
Ban their native tongue
Until it dies.
Making fiction seem as fact
We will teach the Indian how to Act!
We'll lead them away
From ancestral plains,
Decree their day
And change their names.
Oh yes, you can see how the odds are stacked,

We will teach the Indian how to Act!
We must act fast,
We can not wait,
They must forget their past
To assimilate.
Yes, yes, teach the Indian how to Act!
In fewer words, with far less tact
We must teach the Indian not to Act
　. . . so Indian

*Art by
Phil Joe*

Edōsdi / Judith C. Thompson
Tahltan Band - Tahltan and Gitxsan descent

My Grandfather's Cherished Mittens

Tiny beads
so perfectly placed
painting the floral pattern
on the golden canvas.
Swirls of colour—
blues, reds, and greens,
whites, yellows, and silvers.
So tiny, so perfect.

Small pieces of tanned moose hide
adorned with beaver fur.
The inlaying of the thumbs
so tiny, so perfect
so intricately done.

Gold stitching all done by hand.
So tiny, so perfect.
With love sewn into every stitch.

I gaze at my Grandpa's tiny mittens
and think about his mother
working on the mittens while she was carrying him.
so lovingly made for her second born—
the son who would only know her for a fraction of his life.

My grandfather cherished those mittens,
one of the few things he had
to remind him of the mother
he barely remembered.
His mother, Istostē, who passed away
when he was four years old.
He felt love in those mittens,
and in his later years,

he showed off his mittens to as many people as he could.

He gave me those mittens two years before he passed,
before he left us to be with his mother and our Ancestors.
Getting such a gift holds so much meaning.
So much love in those mittens.
So much meaning in the passing on of those mittens.
Grandpa knew I would cherish them almost as much as he did.

When I gaze at those mittens,
I often wonder . . .
what if my grandpa's mother had lived to raise him to adulthood?
How would my grandpa's life have been different?
He most definitely would have been fluent in our traditional language
as his father allowed him to learn the language from Tahltan men
who worked on his ranch.
In his own words, Grandpa said,
"You know,
my mother died when I was four years old.
And what I learned is from the working men.
Tahltans.
If my mother had lived,
I guess I would have spoke it fluently." (personal communication,
December 29, 1999).
With the amazing memory he had for language and numbers,
he would have been an amazing fluent speaker.
Even as a silent speaker,
he could recall words and phrases that others could not.

Grandpa often told me about how,
as a young boy,
his father would let Harry Carlick take him
to potlatches at Drytown,
a short walk from "downtown" Telegraph Creek.
Grandpa would talk about Granny's Uncle Frank,
and how he would open the potlatches by speaking
in the Nisga'a, Lingit, and Kaska languages
even before he would speak in Tahltan,

regardless if people from those Nations were present.
Grandpa would tell me that what Uncle Frank did
showed how much respect our Tahltan people had,
not only for other Nations,
but for their languages as well.

But I wonder . . .
Even if Grandpa had been a fluent speaker of Tahltan,
would he have taught his children?
I would like to think he would have.
But not many people of my mother's generation
learned to speak Tahltan fluently.
Even though our great grandparents and grandparents were fluent
speakers,
our people were made to feel ashamed of our language
due to colonization, assimilation, acculturation.

The mittens symbolize so much to me . . .
The knowledge and wisdom of our Ancestors.
The love between generations.
The slipping away of our language.
The grasping on to our language before it is too late.
And the courageous and tireless work our people are carrying out
In order to keep our language alive.

*Edōsdi /
Judith C.
Thompson
photo*

Connie Merasty
Swampy Cree descent from Opaskwayak Cree Nation

Planting Lies

Mother listless from too many beatings
Father angry from being in school
Sister frightened of the life growing inside her
Still a child herself
Our families ravaged from religion
Where do we go from this shame
These horrific memories keeping us drunk
High without life
Wasted mind diluted with pills
Crank, meth, snow,
Riding a cocaine horse
Untamed by society
Feeling unloved and shunned
This dance of death repeats itself in our family
Forgot victory song a long time ago
Can barely remember yesterday
Street fights and stabbings our legacy
Trafficking young flesh—a trend with inner city angels
Preacher on the corner trying to convert people with no ears
EMT's resuscitating dead souls
Soup lines feed no one's spirit
Stringy old gruel dressed up as meat
Definitely not soul food
Wanting to leave this life but can't find a way out
Walking through the North End
Sore aching feet from no rest
Doorways a welcome rest
Good food years out of our reach

We sing songs to the night sky
Liquored up
With memories of violence dancing through our head
No visitors on this street

Family now but a distant memory
As we lay rotting in rooms of AIDS
Can't see an angel of mercy
Maybe the nuns lied to us
Can't seem to distinguish day or night
The winter days so long and dark
No church to take us in from the cold
Bring me your poor and suffering they preach
Much pain and tears they caused us
And the reason we all live in this hellhole
Did we have children
Maybe left behind like all the people from our rez
Unable to go back to hostile territory
Memories no good
Maybe better days ahead no crossing fingers though
This existence so hard when you have nothing and nowhere to go
Where jail or death is the only future we see
Freedom comes from the end of a needle for many
A bottle of xxx for a cheap time
No actors here in the greatest play on this green
City parks a hidden war zone of drugs and dealers
Wanting someone to pick us up off the sidewalk
Pedestrians never skipping a beat casually ignoring us
My drum beats slowly
No rhythm to my insanity

Pixabay image

Mr. Crow stares at me coldly
From his perch on the hydro line
Waiting to pick off any food left from my meagre breakfast

This day offers no relief from the agony of hunger and addiction
A constant assault of craving running through my veins
A thunderous pounding cracking my already sore head
No mercy on these trails
Waiting on a cool breeze to
Float me away from this torture
Unwilling to let go of this cold spoon
Which I can heat for a nice escape
From the atrocities committed on our bodies
In the name of religion
I have nowhere else to go but these cold dark trails
No wishes come true in this cesspool of pain
Maybe the dark horse of pity will arrive to save me
And my comrades in this endless battle with addiction
Need to find space to sleep now
Hoping the sun will rise to warm my fragile battered shell.

Kevin Bear Henry
Penelakut Tribe; Hul'q'umi'num territories

Careening into the Headlights

From a young age, I was trapped in an unethical system not designed to support Indigenous children. I still feel trapped in an unethical system guided by racism and stereotypical tropes that market Indigenous, Black, and other people of colour as villainous. I have survived a sea of oppressive words—words that ignore the proper development of Indigenous children. I was surrounded by western academics who arrogantly boasted about Indigenous parents being the root of my problems, ignoring the collective traumas Indigenous people carry, which is how colonialism affects every corner of our children and grandchildren's growth and mental health. Over the course of my life, I moved from one foster home to the next foster home; really it was like respite care, only it was in foster home after foster home for nineteen years. I lived like this right up to the institutionalization I suffered inside Jack Ledger Pavilion for "troubled" children labelled with behaviour issues. But I suddenly found myself living in the country and said goodbye to the cornerstones of city life and, hilariously enough, said goodbye to accessible public transit.

I ponder deeply if foster care was my manifest destiny. I know I had access to fresh air, food, clothing, and shelter; yeah, sure, I had shelter, though deep down I knew parts of my soul were still missing. Accessing nature was a plus; I had easy access to lakes, rivers, trails, and wildlife, but it wasn't the same as being able to access my Hul'q'umi'num culture or language. For the most part, I grew up privileged because I was afforded nice foster parents who provided a stable home. So I have no idea of the grim, harsh realities of living on the reservation. No clue at all. I grew up in a city. I grew up in the Western World. It saddens me that I did not grow up in Big Houses. I guess this is the conflict of my life—the life of a city Native wandering two worlds, two spirits, two lives.

I remember being lost in fantasy, seeing myself speak the language of my ancestors. My biggest goals and dreams were of a journey on my bike and seeing myself reach the end of the city limits in hopes of finding Hul'q'umi'num people. I lived by exploring endlessly in hopes any ancestor would take my hand and guide me home. I often ran away from whichever foster or respite home I was placed in; I lingered down by the shores of an ocean my people canoed on. I ran until my body ached all in hopes a spiritual healer would bring me home—not in a western sense of wanting suicide to bring comfort, not in an undertone of craving death to take me—no, I wanted my culture, my language, and my customs to bring me peace. I guess this allowed me to live within the confines of my own imagination and to hide from the hurt and anger festering deep within. The downsides were that I was systematically oppressed—white kids telling me I'm a dirty Indian, while the Indians were telling me I'm an "apple", an Indian without land; an Indian with red skin and a white soul. I will learn much later to call this lateral violence, which is merely a result of colonialism, branching further into neo-colonialism. This is an extension tragically tribally created; one that has elected chiefs and tribal council members who, in my travels, sadly end up unequivocally swearing an oath to honour colonial obligations, irrevocably ignoring ancestral land, culture, and language management.

I awake from this dream; it's a dream of imagining a land or a time where I am free to be Hul'q'umi'num. It's a way to see myself exist far away from the prying eyes of white Canadian-based assimilation tactics. Awaking from these imaginations of freedom feels like spiritual death; without my language and culture, I sometimes feel barely alive spiritually. I'm stuck walking on what were my ancestors' lands, stolen and renamed by western society. I fear my life is but a tough, dusty dirt road which I must saunter in utter despair, wandering with the hopes that I might be able to obtain freedom to feel fully human. Yet I ponder more and more if this dream can be obtainable. The fear to walk this road was the one thing that drove me into fits of rage, anger, and frustration as a youth of colour; crystal meth made complete sense to forget the torment I endured. And not only in my teenage years, perhaps even today I'm continually frustrated and angered because I wandered as a lost soul doomed to hear teachers preach on about how pre-historic Indians are, and this was a classroom discussion I faced just this last semester at UVIC. This much I do know—my anguish became my chains, each link clattering and clanging and taunting my rights to be Hul'q'umi'num. My teachers, doctors, psychiatrists, counsellors, and psychologists are all white people who decided my intellectual levels and behavioural levels; even my levels of rage were decided upon by white people to be too much. If I raged, I was labelled a problematic student. I was pushed into the doors of the Jack Ledger Institution and, later in life, the Eric Martin Institution. What I learned at five years old is that I had to keep submissive to the dominant discourse of the white patriarchy just to survive.

I honestly felt that going back to school as an adult was the move I needed to make in order to better support people on the streets, to grasp colonialism at its roots, and support Indigenous people. I suppose at one point in my life I didn't even know the meaning behind the words, the constructs, the devastations brought about by the western colonization of North America. I'd often learn about my culture when visiting the Mungo Martin Big House as a child, but later I suffered through a flurry of ill-informed white teachers and white students, all with the ill-gotten gains of colonization, peering at the Indian trapped in their classrooms. I was forced to sit in a proverbial glass box, looking on, trapped, and listening to a white western society educating the white masses on the savages they claimed to be fully conquered by a "master race", with no mention of invasion or genocide ever talked about, using textbooks filled with lies written by racists. None of my teachers from my past actually spent time helping me understand residential schooling, Indian hospitals, or the 60s Scoop; yes, punctuation is important, and so is properly and meticulously citing primarily white scholars. But why isn't segregation, racism, and white supremacy properly debated at school, college, or university? Why weren't these topics of depersonalization even within my foster homes, or out in the streets, or even within immigration and refugee policies all over the world? I think this is because of how much western doctrine is pushed weirdly into our minds and how the reality or truth of the world is silenced because of white discourse. I fear we forget just how incredibly powerful we are as Indigenous peoples, as non-white people, as immigrants and refugees leaving ancestral homelands to work hard to survive and provide; we are strength and resiliency full tilt. However, teaching statistics and facts on poverty is a method of theory taught constantly; society blames the poor and destitute I work for today for the problems created and perpetrated by white captains of industry. Interestingly enough, some slight flaws remain within the academic system, and I cannot blame western academia solely for my indiscretions of lacklustre punctuation and grammatical errors that run on and on and on and on within my sentences. Something is missing, but I'm not sure what.

I'm told I should be picking up more books, exercising my brain muscles, or simply asking for help from white authors, writers, poets, instructors. But I find it difficult to say, "I need help!" Mostly because I am weighed down by the oppression crushing my soul. I feel as if I'm being cemented to the floor, but only in reverse, instead of my feet being stuck, my hands become entrenched in the madness of fending off the cemented words that cut the deepest: "unfit mother", "incapable parents/grandparents", "handicapped", "heathen", "he has a lower IQ than most of his white peers", "savage", "squaw", "mindless", "conquered", "pre-historic". I read books from time to time; although, to read a book from time to time is still hard for me. Just to pick up a book and pretend to enjoy reading said book is demoralizing because white scholars remain the dominant discourse. This fact alone causes anguish to flood my veins and consume my heart whole.

I saw my best days spent as a loner. I also had no focus or concentration to get me through the many behavioural schools I was forced into, and all the pre-employment schooling systems offered no comfort for this Indian walking on their own land. Indeed, being institutionalized from a young age is something I blame white society and the foster care system for; judging someone so young without reason other than the colour of their skin has dictated the way I was treated by whites. The way in which I was taught about my existence is now seen as outdated and old fashioned because while teachers called me Indian, I couldn't call them white. I was told how I was being racist toward whiteness for calling people white. Struggling through this sea of "reverse racist" etiquette took me fifteen years to wrestle with; it was a hard truth of a failed school system designed to uplift white students and put down anyone of colour. Colonialism is a method that will blame me for having a top notch, a very consistent strain of fragmented sentences, a mind filled with run-ons, and of constant need for accepting errors textbooks taught me. I'm told these problems within my writing only exist because "English isn't my first language." I looked back at my teacher, laughing, saying, "but I was born with the rhetoric of my colonizer! English is all I know!"

Hul'q'umi'num culture nearly died within those residential schools and those Indian Hospitals. We were turned into relics, gifted hardships, stripped of our languages; my grandparents endured torment for being human. They were dehumanized day in, day out. I realized my eyes were soon floating unnaturally onto these types of ink-soaked pages, and I had to read about my culture from textbooks painting us as godless, to be feared, to be disrespected, to be forgotten, and ignored. In fact, these Indigenous issues within my writing were also the key problem twenty years ago. Because no one white wants to admit to the genocide that came from the hands of their "noble nation." Perhaps my previously failed attempts at writing could also be partially due to my teachers saying I need to think like an Englishman and not with the unnatural thought patterns of a Native—but I am Native! Over the years, I became a professional writer despite teachers telling me that because I'm Indigenous I'll never read, write, or think like my white peers, and I thank a higher power each day since this became true. I watched as my sentence construction followed me around like a bad shadow in the corner of my mind, and there were the terrible grades as well, but I landed a good job—for an Indian, I suppose. How I learn and gather information about my surroundings is and always will be from the perspective of someone partially assimilated into Canadian society. Because for now, in this life, I speak and read English. For me, this was not natural to my development as an Indigenous child or the adult I am today. I have sought help by attending writing workshops in the community in the past, and yet to this day I still have a big issue with starting my writing process, and I find it difficult tracking the essence of my thoughts on paper and keeping my writing flowing, all to the maddening question of "is this grammatically correct?" I often wonder if I just hit my keyboard enough times, in just the right way, that colonization will go away, right?

Michelle Sylliboy
L'nuk (Mi'kmaq)

Meskay nitap (I'm sorry friend)

Meskay nitap (I'm sorry friend) for not saying it
my watch stopped
when you flew by

life cycles emerged slowly without warning trembling at familiar
sounds

how long before
we choose not to suffocate
when flash backs become consistent
escaping nausea
while we re-examine
our faiths of torture
that once permeated
in our skin without any effort

familiar sensations climb
to where magnificence awaits
recognizing sacrifices we took
to arrive at our peaceful
destination at last

Sheena Robinson
Heiltsuk Nation

Grey Skies

Char jumped off the bus at the Patricia Hotel, her worn Chuck Taylors narrowly missing a puddle of vomit. She checked the rest of the sidewalk in front of her. Satisfied that all the gum she saw was old and long ago flattened onto the pavement, she did a quick scan of who was around her, as her mom had taught her to do whenever she was in this neighbourhood. Her dad liked to say that "every day is Halloween in the Downtown Eastside," in hopes that he'd deter Char from visiting as often. Sure, there were lots of people shuffling around here in the DTES, but nobody jumped out at her as extra suspicious.

It was late afternoon in early April, and the sun was trying to break through the marbled clouds before it sank behind the skyscrapers in downtown Vancouver. Several of the Patricia's bar patrons hovered outside the doors to the hotel's pub, smoking. A hunched over woman went up to each of them, asking to buy a cigarette for a quarter. A guy in muddy jeans and work boots gave her a couple of them and was instantly bombarded by other passersby for more. Char chuckled to herself and turned down Dunlevy Street towards Oppenheimer Park.

A woman in a velour, purple tracksuit swayed against the brick wall of the building to the right, eyes closed and mouth open. Her purse lay gaping at her feet, and one hand grasped at the air while the other was balled up in a fist at her side. An older man sat against the same wall a few feet down, his head bobbing in rhythm with the woman but his shoeless feet moving wildly in different directions. Char recognized the signs of a heroin trip and steered wide of them as she passed, but they didn't notice her anyway. As she rounded the corner to her mom's apartment building, she held her breath, then released it noisily when she saw the entrance way clear of people. The buzzer still wasn't working, so she hollered, "Mom!" and waited a few moments before yelling, "Louise!"

The curtains in the window moved, then her mom's pale face peered down at her, frowning at first, then grinning when she recognized her daughter. She motioned to Char to wait, and a few minutes later she appeared at the door, cigarette dangling from her lips and hands fumbling to tie a sweater around her waist. She blew a puff of smoke at Char unintentionally as she opened the lobby door and ushered her inside. Her pupils were large and her fingers were dyed orange from rolling cheap tobacco.

"Hi baby," Louise said gruffly. She cleared her throat, then reached in for a hug. "Come upstairs." She tousled Char's hair, which was cut quite short and dyed black with purple streaks. "How did you get that raven black hair when I'm so blonde, anyways?"

Char followed her mom to the stairs. "The elevator is *still* broken?"

Her mom threw her hands up as she started up the stairs. "You don't even know. It's been like this for months. The sink and the tub are both leaking nonstop too. And the roaches!" She looked back at Char. "I mean, the halls. They don't clean them. It's disgusting. I'm sorry."

When they arrived on the fifth floor, Char was glad she didn't have to use the bathroom. Her mom shared one with the whole floor, and it was only cleaned once a day, usually in the morning. By now it had been used by many different people for many different reasons, the least of them being to pee, most likely.

They entered the small cubicle that was supposed to be a bachelor suite, the room her mom had called home for the past six months. Louise went to the table and cleared it quickly, throwing things into a plastic bag and shoving it in a corner. Char made a point not to look at what her mom was putting away. She didn't want to know.

She sat on the edge of the single bed, slinging her backpack onto the floor. Her mom took the only chair.

"Sorry it's such a mess," she said, waving her hand around absently. It wasn't actually messy, though, because her mom didn't have enough belongings to clutter anything up. Everything was just sort of old and run down. There was a small sink, a heating element, a very small counter, four cupboards, a mini fridge, and a small desk with Louise's beloved computer on it. There was no closet, only a small set of drawers and a garbage bag full of clothes next to it. There was a throw rug under Char's feet. The only thing Louise had brought from their home was a dreamcatcher that she'd bought on a road trip to Alberta long ago, which hung in the window. That was it. They both lit smokes.

"How's your dad?" Louise asked after a few silent minutes.

"He's good, I guess. He thinks I'm at work right now though."

"I didn't know you found a job!" said Louise, her face lighting up. "That's great, Char!"

Char looked down at her hands. "I didn't actually, yet," she stammered. "I just told him that to get him out of my hair." She had told him that, actually, so he wouldn't think she was coming to see her mom all the time. Greg had found Louise partying again in their living room with a group of people he didn't know when he had come home from work early one day, and he had kicked them out. Louise never came back that time. He had forbidden Char to visit her when she'd landed this place in the heart of the DTES. Sometimes it was as if he'd forgotten that he used to party too.

"Oh, Charlotte." Her mom's mood changed instantly. She wasn't mad, but she was disappointed, which was worse. "You're not going to make money taking photos or writing poems, girl. Smarten up."

Char had just been about to reach into her backpack to show her mom her latest scrapbook, which featured black and white photos of the various Indigenous residents she had encountered in the DTES. Something about them made her feel closer to her culture, even though they were from all different nations. These people each had a story, something they were running from, or to. She had interviewed some of them and written poems about her favourites. Char was raised away from the reserve her dad had grown up on and had missed out on living off the land and learning her language. She had no Elders to talk to or learn from growing up, and some of the old Natives from the park had started to fill that gap lately.

She became aware of the silence that had fallen upon the tiny room when there was a quick, quiet knock on the door. Louise jumped up and opened the door, but not enough for Char to see who it was. She heard them talking lowly and watched her mom reach out of her back pocket and pull out a rolled up ten dollar bill and hand it to whoever was in the hall. As she closed the door, she mumbled something about her neighbour asking to borrow money until tomorrow, but Char had seen her slip something in her front pocket. "Hey, mom, do you want to have a game of crib?" Louise had taught it to Char long ago, and it was their favourite way to pass the time. At least it used to be. Her mom had become more and more reclusive lately, and the time they spent together was limited to this tiny room.

"You know what, honey, I'm really not feeling that great. I think I need a nap or something. Maybe you could come back tomorrow?" she said. She looked out the window as some crows suddenly started cawing nonstop. *Craw! Craw!* Her forehead creased. "It's getting dark, anyway, and I don't want you down here after dark."

It wasn't, but Char took the hint. She sighed. "Alright, mom. See you later. Maybe we can go for a walk tomorrow if you're feeling better." She grabbed her backpack and leaned in for a hug, but Louise had turned to rummage through the plastic bag she'd tossed in the corner.

Char had told her dad she was working at a restaurant as a dishwasher and would be home late, so she had quite a bit of time to kill. The crows were still cawing loudly and fluttering around frantically as she walked out of her mom's apartment. She looked down to see a baby crow crouching low to the ground. She bent down to see if it was injured, then saw that its beak was missing—in its place a screaming red hole. She quickly recoiled her hand and ducked as a crow, maybe one of its parents, aggressively dive bombed her.

Reaching into her backpack, Char fumbled for her camera. She shrieked as one of the crows swooped down at her again, actually grabbing some of her hair in its claws this time. Working quickly, she snapped a few shots of the young corvid, its eyes closed, shoulders hunched against the pain of this harsh world. Char wanted to help the poor thing, but she didn't know how.

She remembered back when she had been a young girl, and her dad had rescued an abandoned baby crow from the park. He had excitedly called her out to the shed where he had set up her old rabbit's cage for it with a blanket, a bowl of water, and some bird seed. He wasn't working at the time, and this was an exciting project for him. Looking back now, Char had to laugh at how they'd wondered why it didn't want the birdseed. It wasn't a chickadee. Her mom had laughed at him, saying he didn't deserve to be part of the Raven clan after that. He didn't find it funny.

Craw! Craw! Char looked up to the crows, now perched on the telephone wire above her. They were looking up though, and her gaze followed theirs into the granite sky. Hundreds of crows were flying southeast above them, making their way to their nightly meeting at Grandview Park. Every evening, like clockwork, crows from all over the Lower Mainland gathered at this one tree in Burnaby to have a meeting. Char watched as one of the crows looked down at its broken child, cawed at its partner, and flew up to join its contemporaries.

Char slowly stood up and thought about how her dad had withdrawn after the baby crow had died. For weeks, he lay in bed with the curtains drawn and the small TV on his dresser blasting sports games and highlights twenty-four hours a day. Louise had slept on the couch, gratefully it seemed in retrospect, and sneaked out to party a lot of the nights. Char ate toast and cereal until the cupboards were bare and her dad had finally emerged and gone to get groceries. The next day she heard him on the phone talking to his aunt, crying about something that had happened long ago.

A few days later Char sat in her room working on her scrapbook. As she sifted through the black and white portraits, she thought about the stories each picture told her. Every one of them had a reason for ending up in Vancouver's poorest area. They may have looked rough to a lot of people, but that was because nobody bothered to know their stories, Char thought to herself.

There was a knock on her bedroom door and her dad popped his head in. "Hey kiddo, no work tonight?"

Char tried to cover the photos with the scrapbook. "Uh, no, not tonight."

Her dad smiled and sauntered over to her desk. "Homework, then?" he said, but his smile fell when he saw the corner of a photo of Max, her favourite Elder down at the park. "Char, this guy lives in the slums. Those people can't be trusted!" He folded his arms against his chest. "It's not safe for you to be running around down there with all the druggies and drunks and mentally insane people. Including your mom."

"They're people, just like me. And you. They're just lost."

"They're not like me."

"Could have been."

His throat pulsated with words he couldn't seem to muster, then he turned and walked out of the room, closing the door behind him.

Char stared out the window to their backyard. A single tear rolled down her cheek. She blinked and tried to focus on anything but this moment. She wished she'd known the rest of her family but her dad wouldn't talk about them. Suddenly a raven flew into the yard and landed on the fence. They didn't usually come into the city like this. *Croak! Croak!* It seemed to be looking right at her. The raven called out a couple more times, then flapped its wings and took off down the darkening alley. Fat raindrops began to fall. Char sighed and put her head down on her arms and closed her eyes against the night.

Art by Leanna Raven Paul

Sharai Mustatia
photo

"This image was taken after I was renovicted in 2015, from a house I had planned on living in for the rest of my life. That eviction caused my homelessness for nearly four months. It is shot as a multiple exposure of my old neighbourhood mixed with other neighbourhoods unfamiliar. The Inukshuk gave me hope that I would find a home even though I was feeling most lost and hopeless."
~Sharai Mustatia

Darlene McIntosh
Elder – Lheidli T'enneh Nation

Opening Prayer

CREATOR . . .

Thank you for this beautiful day on Mother Earth . . .
thank you for the gift of community . . .

Thank you for bringing all who are present . . .
ready and willing to work towards building a strong working relationship
with the children . . . and most important . . . willing to make a powerful
commitment to the kids in care . . .

With this commitment, we walk the good red road in promoting and
acknowledging our unique differences in how we as a community deeply
care for the children who need love and protection, and we need to
sustain all that is needed for their well being . . .

CREATOR . . .

We come together to celebrate our young people who have received
the support needed . . . whatever that may be . . .
let us all come together as "ONE"
bringing the best of who we are into the world . . .

MOTHER EARTH . . .

As we stand on you softly, connecting with your
Heartbeat . . .
thank you for continuing to support us . . .
allowing your essence to vibrate through us . . .
interconnecting with all that live in and on your body.

CREATOR . . .

Thank you for celebrating with us today . . .
thank you for leading us gently on our journey back to you . . .
let us be guided by your light . . .

Closing Prayer

Dear Creator . . .
Grandfathers and Grandmothers . . .

As this beautiful winter day comes to a close . . .
thank you for all that has taken place today . . .
Thank you for all the participation . . .
Thank you for all the knowledge and wisdom shared . . .

As the winds bring a change of weather . . .
they also bring a change
of how to do the best practices for our Aboriginal peoples . . .

We thank Creator for guiding us on the good red road of instituting
plans
that will work on making us whole in all aspects of who we are . . .

As the sun is high in the sky, warming us in the coolness of the northern
energy . . .
it touches our Spirit . . .
asking us to come into the wisdom of our Hearts . . .

We thank Mother Earth for allowing us to walk softly on her . . .
leaving no footprints . . .

May all those present,
go home knowing that what they received today . . .
will benefit all . . .

Creator
We ask that you keep our people safe tonight . . .
and may tomorrow be a good day . . .

Creator . . . hear our prayer . . .

All my relations . . .
mussi

Natasha McCarthy
Ucluelet First Nation (Nuu Chah Nulth); (Cree and Wet'suwet'en on mother's side)

Searching

Disconnection is what I feel—disconnection to those around me, to my ancestors before me, and to my spirit. I must find the answer. As I make my way into the wilderness, I smell the damp moss, I feel the ferns hit my legs, I feel the cedars brush my arms, and I hear the subtle sound of dried leaves crunching under toe. I feel that the real me is somewhere in these woods. I must search for my spirit to come back from some distant realm. Listening intently for a moment, not creating my own assault on the stillness around me, I can hear all the things I have forgotten. At first, I hear the usual boisterous sounds: a bird, a squirrel, and even small bugs. Listening even more intently, I hear the fluttering of leaves trickling down from the tops of the unknown. I feel the softness, the warmth, and the reality of the natural world around me. But the struggle I face is listening to my body and feeling my connection to the earth, while fighting with all the worries, fears, and anger of my everyday life.

I open my eyes. I feel the sun's rays peeking through the canopy above. The love and warmth from the sun become visible on my skin—a constant reminder to how grateful I am for the existence of light, and all that it brings. In our overloaded, overstimulating society, I am not able to see all the real colours around me. Here in the woods, I see a beautiful kaleidoscope of greens, browns, and reds that I am now capable of recognizing again. In nature, the differences are much more brilliant and vivid, existing in a perfect balance, undisturbed. From the highly pigmented fern on my right leg to the subtleness of the cedar bow on my shoulders, I become more aware. Staring out from my tiny place in the world, I can see every living being around me, reaching, straining, begging for a piece of the light. The slow, constant movements of the rays on the trees from above remind me of the gentle breeze blowing. I become lost in the movement of rays and sway of trees and branches until I feel at peace.

The wind quietly echoes and gathers strength when it beats through the terrain around me, and then it reaches my bare skin, triggering goosebumps. Shocking me and suddenly placing me back in my spot in this open lair of wilderness. Gurgling stomach and goosebumps remind me that if nothing else, I am human. The need for warmth and comfort come to the forefront of my mind, so I take off my pack and gather my thoughts. First, I must create a fire pit with earth and stone, and then I look around and find the sacred directions to create an altar in the east. I grasp small pine needles from the floor, small twigs, and some shavings from a small birch branch, making a bundle from all of my surroundings. Bending over, sparks in hand, I create a wall of warmth from the chill of the surrounding wild. With smoke engulfing me, I drop my bundle of kindling and feel the cold releasing from my body. I feel the twinge of hunger, and again I remember why I came here in the first place; I came here to fast. I am here to find my spirit and be reunited once again. I look at the pack my mother packed for me, and I can feel her prayers for me pouring out of the top as I open it. Inside I find a blanket for sleeping; sage, and an abalone bowl for prayers; tobacco, for offerings; and a red bundle all on its own. I feel the strong energy surging from the bundle of red; I hear whispers coming from it. I'm too terrified of its power to open it. I do not think I am strong enough. I know what it is, I know what I must do, but fear keeps me frozen here, staring at the red cloth bundle.

Something strong stirs inside of me almost screaming to open the bundle, but the stirring does not force my hand. I sit by the warmth of the fire with the whispers behind me. The sun begins to descend to the west of my little camp, and an incredible need takes over my body, and I cannot resist opening the bundle any longer. I bend over and gently open the bundle on the small altar I created next to my fire. I pull out my ash container first, then my mother's medicine pouch. Lastly, I stare at the people's pipe. I feel it staring back at me—the whispers have turned into loud voices, and now I hear their songs. I still resist packing the bowl and beginning the ceremony as my mother had taught me, for I fear what awaits me on the other side.

I ignore the calling, the pull that I feel from the sacred pipe, choosing to listen to my fear instead. I lie at the fire's side and wait for sleep to take me. I hear the pipe go silent and look around me. All is very still, even the air has ceased to pierce my skin with its frosty bite. The stars above become brighter, and they slowly begin to move, deliberately circling above. The stars become a vibrant, stunning vortex over my head. The swirl moves faster and faster until all the stars in the sky have become one in a huge glowing orb of starlight. The orb shoots out of the sky and lands gracefully right beside me. Within a blink of the eye the orb is gone, and there stands a perfect woman, wearing all white. She is tall with long black hair. I look closer, and I see she has the kind eyes of my grandmother and the smile of my mother.

This spirit has come to bring me home, to find peace within; out of respect, I do not question her. She steps forward and places her hand on my heart and smiles knowingly at me. I feel an instant relief come over me. This gesture is the familiar, loving, gentle touch of my auntie. The reason why I was fearful of the spirits was now touching my heart. I feel the love pulsating from her spirit hand to my lost heart. She takes my hand and we walk over to my blanket and sit together; she looks at me as though I should speak first. I refrain from speaking out of shock or fear that if I say the wrong thing she might leave me again. My mother's smile illuminates her face, and I breathe easier; I see her chest rise as she takes a deep breath.

We sit in silence on the blanket for what feels like hours, and she holds my hand in hers with her soft but deliberate touch. I know she is about to speak, so I listen for her wisdom, trying my best to be open to the words. She asks me one simple question. I know what is coming, but still I fear disappointing her. Her voice echoes through my soul. "My daughter, I have come to you to ask why you strayed off the red road?" I feel my voice quiver. "I was angry at the spirit world. Why would you take her from me?" I begin to feel the heat of anger growing inside. "I still needed her! Why should I forgive you for taking her?" I scream at her. Embarrassed by my overly emotional outburst, I wait for her to react and try not to make eye contact. The spirit looks at me with understanding eyes, and with a serene voice she says, "we know how much love you had for her. We know how much you miss her." A wave of calm comes over my body, causing me to take a deep breath and feel connected to the earth again—grounded. She looks at me, I can almost see my reflection in her deep brown black eyes, and she says, "but you also must know she would not have wanted you to leave the red road out of anger." I cannot bring myself to say anything; all I am able to do is nod. She is right; I have been running away from the pain out of anger.

We sit in stillness again, I let her words sink in, I feel unspeakable pain from the loss of my beloved auntie once again. I let out my tears of agony, and I smell the sweet scent of sage burning in the shell—the smoke washes over my body and soul. She lovingly wipes my tears away, whispering prayers over me as she does so. I open my eyes. She gestures toward the pipe, and before I know what I am doing, her spirit compels me to move toward it. I pick up the delicate people's pipe in my left hand; I feel the vibrations to my heart. I take the medicine pouch in my other hand. I walk back to the smudge bowl and cleanse both the pouch and the pipe. I hand them to the spirit and she packs the bowl, saying silent prayers to Mother Earth, to Father Sky, to the four directions, and all the spirits. I watch as she takes an ember from the fire with her bare hand and lights the sacred pipe; she inhales the medicine deep into her lungs. She blows the sacred smoke to the earth, the sky, and the four directions, and then she blows some over herself and spins the pipe toward me. I cannot refuse this from a spirit, I tell myself. I know I must do this. I know this is what I need. I do the same for myself, following step by step what she has done. We pass the pipe back and forth for what seems like hours; finally, the bowl empties.

Once she empties the ashes into a pouch of her own, she tells me why the single bowl lasted so long. "This ceremony was to bring out your pain and cleanse you of all the burdens that you carry with you," she says. I notice a small, white, child-like shadow behind her, and I can't help but stare at this small child; she is beautiful and innocent. The spirit looks at me then at the shadow child and smiles at her, patting the child's head. The spirit takes my hand and brings the shadow child and me together; the child looks so familiar, and I want to hold her like she is my own. "This is your innocent spirit," the spirit says to me. "She has been with you for your entire life. She knows all of the trauma you have endured. When your auntie passed away and you walked away from the red road, you shut this innocent child out." I nod and understand why this child is so familiar; thinking back on my life, I have always felt her presence. The shadow child and I stare at each other for a long time, until I finally summon the courage to speak again. "Can you forgive me?" I say to the child. She does not speak to me; she only runs into my arms and then disappears inside of my body. I cannot explain the feeling of being whole after so many years of being half of a person, but that is how I feel.

Suddenly, I wake and it is morning. The fire died long ago, and the sun has just begun to rise. I rush over to the altar I had made yesterday and begin the pipe ceremony without fear and with the knowledge I no longer must fear that I am alone. I hear elusive movements behind me, but I do not need to look—I know the shadow child is with me once again.

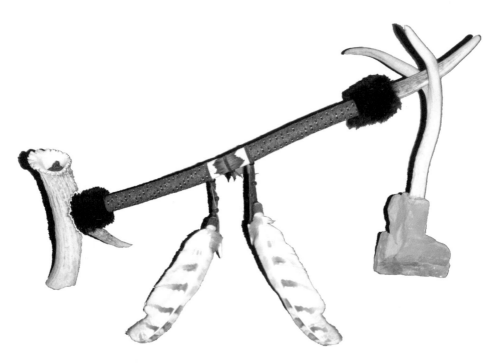

Pipe from the Alan Robertson collection

Shauntelle Dick-Charleson
Hesquiaht and Songhees

I Was There

So in order for me to graduate high school
I have to learn the curriculum for math, science, English, and social
studies
I also have to learn someone else's culture
And learn a second language

In order for me to succeed in life
I have to learn someone else's culture
And learn a second language

In order for me to get a good job, a marriage, and a house
I have to learn someone else's culture
And learn a second language

And some kid in my class says, "But you don't have to pay taxes,
do you?"

What?

And Why
Am I supposed to learn *his* culture
If I barely know my own

Why am I supposed to learn *his* language
I don't even know my first language

So, to him I say, let me be your teacher for a second

In the 1870s, the settlers,
Well, the priests and nuns,

Took kids to school
Well, took them from their families
To educate them
Well, to teach them a culture that wasn't theirs, stripping them of
their identity

These children were abused mentally and physically
They were shamed for their skin
Because they were different from the nuns and priests, different from
the white kids

And in 1996
The last residential schools were closed down

But that didn't mean the shaming stopped

It didn't mean that they
—I mean we—
Were done being abused

The First Nations people were put on a small, specific piece of land
Because the Canadian government wanted to separate us from others

So

Am I supposed to thank them for the reserve I live on?
Am I supposed to thank them for leaving me and my family a bit of
land?
That has no streams, no fish, no trees. Because those things
matter to me
I know what you're thinking
Why is she talking?
It doesn't even affect her
She wasn't even there

But No I was there
I was there when the father whipped my grandpa

I was there when the sister took my grandma's hair away from her
I was there when they told my ancestors that they were savages
I was there when they took my Native tongue away

I'm sorry if I disrespected your father

Actually, no I'm not because he disrespected mine first

And don't tell me to shut up because I've stayed quiet for too damn long

I want you to hear my voice because they wouldn't hear theirs

I can't tell you the things that my ancestors were feeling
But I know that they're still healing

They are looking down on my generation, and they're still grieving
because
I don't know my language
I don't really know my culture
So how could I know myself

So, yes, I was there

I was there when they took my Native tongue away
I was there

Michelle Sylliboy
L'nuk (Mi'kmaq)

Rock Salt

I rise above the clouds daily calmly oblivious to unnecessary antidotes
as waves enter my space of contentment

feel glad feel small within the confines of a universe that swallows you
on a daily basis

compliments to the Creator for bringing us a new day reminding us to
stay true making memories like a tourist on a new adventure

before we can turn around with a new sigh she devours me with
sweetness rock salt fresh air crashing into each other like lovers on a
first date

Michelle Sylliboy photo

Hank Charles
Lac La Ronge Indian Band

Embracing the Source of Our Existence:
A Tribute to the Survivors of Residential Schools

I have always been drawn to the river for as long as I can remember.
I could sit quietly for hours and listen to the sounds of the seagulls,
ducks, geese, and other birds that depend on water as the source of
their existence. I would watch them glide gracefully down and land on
the surface of the rushing river flow. Eagles watching intently from
tree tops. The flutter of feathers as pelicans fly off to feast on top of
rocks, standing majestically, heads held high, watching intently across
the river scape for the next fish that gives up their life so they can
survive for another day. Screaming seagulls fighting, playing, and having
conversations. Splashing water. There is rhythm to the sound of the land,
lakes, and rivers in northern Saskatchewan. I sit in a trance-like state,
nourished by the energies, allowing the sun, wind, and sounds to do their
work in bringing me back to a sense of balance. I am part of this land,
and the land is part of who I am.

My name Hank Charles. I am a member of the Lac La Ronge Indian
Band. I am an Intergenerational Survivor of Residential School. When
people began to talk about Intergenerational Survivors, I was not fully
aware what that meant. Like other First Nations across the county, many
of my people were forced into the Residential School system as children.
It is only recently I have begun to think about this whole collective
experience. It finally occurred to me I was an Intergenerational Survivor.
However, I did not have the slightest clue what that meant in my own
life. I would hear stories, but I was not able to make a connection
of what the impacts were in my family. Like so many people in my
generation, the real history was never taught in schools, only whispers
within the community as if not to offend anyone and most especially
those who had converted into the faith that had attempted to destroy
them in the first place. Normalization was entrenched so very carefully.

I think to myself, how these institutions were in place for 100 years. There are those who remember and can speak of the harms committed, and there are those who choose to remain silent for reasons of their own. Forgiveness has many shades. Meanwhile, I struggle to know. I struggle to understand. I struggle to bring the pieces together. There is something there that is profound. My heart knows and it is unsettling. My mind, however, is distracted by other things in life like surviving for another day.

Beginning in the 1880s and for 100 years, Canada's federal government initiated an assimilation education policy that took several generations of children from their families and placed them in Residential Schools (Milloy, 1999; TRC 2012:2015). They were disconnected from the land, communities, and traditional knowledge teachers, who were the source of their worldview, cultures, values, knowledge systems, languages, and spiritual beliefs. There were eighteen residential schools in the province of Saskatchewan alone. The policy was to tear down the child and make them into the likeness of European settlers. Many suffered horrific physical, emotional, and sexual abuse. Experiments were conducted on them (Mosby, 2013). Hundreds died in these schools, and there are gravesites adjacent to the buildings. There was a massive loss of cultures and languages. Some scholars look at the experiences as cultural genocide and outright genocide (McDonald & Hudson, 2012). When the Truth and Reconciliation Report on Residential Schools came out in 2015, I could not find any Calls to Action regarding Intergenerational Survivors. The social and psychological impacts are still observable in First Nation communities across Canada. I see the devastation in my own community of Lac La Ronge Indian Band. The challenges and struggle to repair the damage starts from within our homelands. Every family needs to make a serious and comprehensive impact assessment. The members from my band have made a lot of progress, but there is still a long way to go.

My mind drifts back with a focus on my family. We come from such a rich, vibrant, and beautiful northern Cree culture with traditional stories that guide how we think and how we relate to others including the natural world (Brightman, 1989). We are taught to respect others regardless of race, culture, and other social markers. The same spirit that flows through me is the same spirit that flows through all humans, and so how can I be the 'other' when the 'other' is a part of who I am? I cannot imagine what my late father, Gilbert Edwin Roberts, and other members of my community had to endure in these institutions. I look at my own son and think how devastated I would be if something were to happen to him. My anger swells up. I have a right to my own thoughts and feelings. I am only human. My late father was once a little boy himself. He was born into a world of hunters, trappers, fishermen, and gatherers. It is probably the reason why I am so attracted to the land, lakes, and rivers. It is where I find peace. It is where I find solace. It is where I can have safe conversations with myself in my own way, in my own time, without outside pressures. The power of the natural world is healing. As I begin to make sense of the impacts of the Residential School system in my own life, I realize what happened to my father and other family members was not their fault. I also realize now that I suffered childhood trauma because of that system. Like other Intergenerational Survivors, I was exposed to the violence, alcohol, anger, times of hunger, and all sorts of unspeakable ugliness. Somewhere along the way I picked up some of that anger. I have personal life challenges, but I have learned to forgive. I have slowly begun to let go of the baggage that was not mine to begin with. I know the grand narrative now. I know now where it all came from. I have to pick up the chips where they have fallen and make amends where I can. However, I also have to remember the positive aspects of my childhood that give me hope. I have to make good memories to replace all the bad ones. We all have to do that.

My late father was a hard worker and very humble. He did the best he could despite what he went through in Residential School. I remember him taking me out on the land to hunt and trap in the winter. He had his way of teaching me as a growing boy even though at the time it seemed excessive. He was preparing me for the real world. I would watch him. Cree children are taught very early to develop keen observation skills. Trapper kids are tough. I would hike for miles on end in the deepest of snow. He taught me basic survival skills; how to build shelters; make a fire; search for edible wild foods, berries, and plants. My father was a good hunter and tracker. He could shoot a moose clear across the lake. There was a softness in him and the deepest of love for my late sister Angel who passed away from lupus. He was a good singer and guitar player. I picked up my love for music from both him and my late brother

Virgil Bird, who died tragically on the streets of Prince Albert. I think every trapper wants to pass on their knowledge and skills to the next generation of youth so they don't forget who they are and where they come from. I am grateful that my father was able to do that for me.

As Intergenerational Survivors, we too have stories to share. Though we suffered in different ways, what we went through cannot be taken lightly. Children are not supposed to be hurt in any shape or form. In order to make an assessment of the impacts, I have to think of the multi-dimensional and multi-layer impacts, beginning at the individual level and outward within my family, community, and nation (Michell, 2015). I have to think about the mental, spiritual, emotional, and physical impacts. It is never ending. The hatred of the oppressor was unleashed into families and communities like a winter blizzard—cold, brutal, and unwavering. Survivors, with layer after layer of grief and loss, came out of that system with no supports in place for them to deal with the aftermath. Some still have no idea what the impacts are. It is still very hard for me to understand too. But I am trying. That's all I can do. Memory flashbacks come and go like birds gliding in and out of the river waterways. I know we are entering a metaphoric springtime. I see young people so full of life today. There are so many successes. These are our role models and the next generation of nation builders. I watch the river and allow my problems, hurt, anger, shame, and fears to float away. The land is the healer and teacher.

Today, I have hope. I am beginning to understand. We take small steps. I know I will never fully heal. Perhaps the next generation will have that opportunity. This is where my heart is at this point in my life. I want to make a difference in the lives of others, especially young people who themselves are Intergenerational Survivors. This is where the flow of my healing comes from. I am told by Elders that we must go back to the land in order to heal from the impacts of these institutions. I strongly believe that. My dream is to create a land-based excursion initiative where I can take both Indigenous and Non-Indigenous peoples onto the land, lakes, and rivers so that I can share the beauty of my Cree culture. I want to demonstrate resilience in an era of reconciliation. We have given so much to this country despite everything that happened to us. I have family members who have served in the Canadian Armed Forces, including myself, fighting for the same fundamental human rights that all citizens enjoy today. Sadly, several of my young relatives have committed suicide as a result of intergenerational trauma and cultural confusion. It frightens me to the core. There are times I feel helpless in not knowing what I can do to make a difference. It doesn't matter what race you are. I want to help both Indigenous and Non-Indigenous young people. There are survivors who are trying to heal within the confines of four walls, encased in a tomb without an outlet. For me, it is the land, lakes, and rivers in my traditional territories where I find freedom to express and be nourished by the natural world. I breathe out the negative and breathe in life-giving energies. I look around and see the beauty of the land. If we can internalize this awesomeness, we can see the beauty in others. That's where it all begins. As Intergenerational Survivors, we must embrace the source of our existence—the land, the giver of life.

References

Brightman, R.A. (1989). *Acaoohkiwina and Acimowina: Traditional narratives of the Rock Cree Indians*. Regina, Saskatchewan: Canadian Plains Research Center

Elias, B., Mignone, J., Hall, M., Hong, S., Hart, L., & Sareen, J. (2012). Trauma and suicide behaviour histories among a Canadian Indigenous population: An empirical exploration of the potential role of Canada's residential school system. *Social Science and Medicine, 74(2012)*, 1560-1569.

MacDonald, D., & Hudson, G. (2012). The genocide question and Indian Residential Schools in Canada. *Canadian Journal of Political Science, 45(2)*, June, 427-449.

Michell, H. (2015). *Shattered spirits in the land of the little sticks: Contextualizing the impact of Residential Schools among the Woodland Cree*. Vernon, B.C.: JCharlton Publishing Ltd.

Milloy, J. (1999). *A national crime: The Canadian government and the residential school system*. Winnipeg, Canada: University of Regina Press.

Mosby, I. (2013). Administering colonial science: Nutrition research and human biomedical experimentation in Aboriginal communities and residential schools, 1942-1952. *Social History, XLVI (91)*, May 2013.

TRC. (2012). *They came for the children*. Ottawa, ON: A report prepared for the government of Canada.

TRC. (2015). Honouring the truth, reconciling for the future: A summary of the final report of the TRC. Ottawa, ON: A report prepared for the government of Canada.

Charla Lewis
Coast Salish, Squamish

Wind Wisdom

Have you heard the whispers of the Wind?
If you listen, you may hear Her wisdom,
Telling tales of long ago.
Her warm, gentle breeze,
Carrying the redolence of an immemorial Sunrise.
Of tawny bodies dancing across ripe lands,
Stomping, praising feet, raising the Earth.
Of billowing smoke and thunderous drums,
Beckoning primordial voices to speak.
Of ancient oral traditions and sacred song,
Steeped in the Earth; calling Creator to commune with them.
Of Women convening with the Moon,
And Men racing with the Sun.
Of wild, untethered
Freedom.
The Wind, She remembers this;
A bursting joy She cannot contain, a ceaseless laughter,
Carrying through time as a boundless echo.
She laughs. But, too, She cries.
Have you heard the weepings of the Wind?
Harrowing, sorrowful howls,
A desperate gale of sadness,
Breaking the empty quiet of night.
Her cold chill,
Carrying the bitter, biting gust of mal-intent.
Of closed, calloused minds and violent ambition,
Billowing in the sails of wayward ships.
Of brown bodies littered across the lands they nurtured,
Blood soaking the Earth; calling to Creator to reconcile.
Of proud, glorious regalia,
Stripped, stolen, and replaced as costume.
Of children hiding under stairs, in hidden rooms, in mothers' arms;
Caught! In one fell swoop removed.
Of Women missing and murdered,
And Men cast into a dark, seething void.

Of savage, cruel
Colonization.
The Wind, She remembers this;
A deep, hollow pain She cannot contain.
Holding fast every moment that has been,
She carries the bittersweet scent of both joy and sorrow.
She pulls the past, as a thread, through the eye of the present,
Weaving it into the fabric of the future;
A billowing tapestry of time—lest we forget.
Listening ever so quietly,
We may hear the Wind telling tales of what is to come;
A distant beating drum, ceaseless and strong.
Reverberations:
Of Restoration, of Reclamation,
Of Reconciliation to the time of Freedom.
Such is the Wisdom of the Wind,
If you listen.

*Art by
Phil Joe*

Sharai Mustatia
Métis/Cree/Romanian – Coast Salish Territory

Protection

She asked me would i
be with Her when Her Baby was born
yes
i said your invitation honours me
my Heart broke in fear
my own losses
try to stop my Love
but courage
but bravery
and self doubt
and i go anyway
when She calls
i drop everything and leave immediately
driving for hours
to get to Her
to Her coming baby
to keep my promise
to be there
for Her and Her Child
She a Full Blooded Indian
me
Mixed
She needed someone there
to keep watch over the white midwife
who wanted to not be there at all
we breathed together
we cried and laughed together
and too many hours later her Son was born
a Beautiful Indigenous Baby Boy.
someone told me i was
a Doula
but i don't know about that
i just followed my Instincts and my Heart
to protect an Indigenous Mother

from scrutiny and judgment
to protect her Motherhood and tell Her all along
especially when She was crying loudest
wanting to surrender
that She is a Good Mother
A Strong Mother
A Worthy Mother
Lovable and full of Love
and She deserves to keep Her Son.

Skeena Reece
Tsimshian/Gitksan and Cree/Métis

Response to Protection

what a beautiful and heartbreaking honour
I wonder how it must have been for her
an indigenous woman with white skin
her babies are gone and not by her choice
it is never by 'her' choice
sitting with me
watching over me
my baby writhing inside
waiting to get outside
I fear what it will be like for him out here
a place that doesn't want him
doesn't want his mother
to even be alive
let alone outside
but there is love here
as is reflected by the eyes of my witnesses
she can see me
she can see him
and that's all that matters
right now
till it's safe
we will work tirelessly
until it is
safe

Dennis Saddleman
Nlaka'pamux Nation, Coldwater Band

Those Children

(The Spirits of Residential School, some people call them Ghosts)

Look at those children
There's a whole bunch of them
They came from that red brick building
Those children
Those boys and girls, they walked in silence
Silence, it clung to untold stories
Those children, their voices faded
Their voices faded when the eyes of sin
Eyes of sin stared at them

Look at those children
They came from that red brick building
Those children separated from their families
Separated from their childhood
Separated from their dolls and teddy bears
Those children, those children with worn out shoes
Those children, they were skin and bones
Those children, they walked back and forth
They had no paths
No roads
No destination
Look at those children
They came from that red brick building
Those children

They're spirits of grief
They're spirits of the past
Those children
They're looking for prayers

Looking for freedom
Looking for hope
With heartache and sadness
With heartache and tears
I watch those children, they all walk back
Walk back to the red brick building
They all enter the red brick building
Those children
I dread
I dread
Those children will be forgotten
Those children will never return home

BiblioArchives / LibraryArchives

Joanne Arnott
Métis

The Bouquet of Night

I.
Between the solitary promise of the death of the 'born alone, dies alone'
island of a man

The one who has no mother from which he is born, the one who god
and capital made and remade

And the painful shared insult of mass graves
Whole populations perishing, buried too quickly to know 'who' and
'whom,'
only 'them' 'us'

There is the die-hard diplomacy and romanticism
'Never leave me' 'I won't'

II.
In the afterworld
I lean in for a kiss
You are as dusty as I am, together

Waiting for the sun to shine on us again
The feel of rain on skin, the feel of skin
The taste of your breath, the taste of breath

The scent of fresh linen and you, together
The scent of me and the feel of a freshly washed blanket

The bouquet of night

Michael Calvert
Mid-Island Métis Nation

All My Relations

"Moushoum, tell us another story," pleaded the children sitting around Thomas Hamelin. He sat silently in the shade of the ancient oak, thinking of what their next lesson might be. The young ones edged closer. The morning sun lit the tips of the valley's tall Spruces and Cedars in a way it only did once summer had moved on. Smoke trailed from a log smokehouse nearby, where salmon were dried in preparation for winter. This was the twenty-seventh fall the Elder had lived in the valley, choosing to live the old ways. There were only seven of them back then. Thomas recalled his moushoum and one of the many stories his grandfather had told him.

"I will share with you one of my favourites," he said. "The story of the last beaver."

The contented young ones sat back and settled in for another of grandfather's stories.

"Once, beavers were abundant and ruled much of Turtle Island, shaping the land to their will and controlling where the other animals could live. Beavers were powerful creatures, but they, like we humans, could be greedy. One family of beavers could transform this entire valley into a lake."

Thomas paused and let the children take in the expanse of the valley. Several mouths hung open as the younger ones imagined that feat.

"This greed made the beavers easy to find, for their fur was coveted by the colonizers in the time of the Ancestors. By the time the trapping of beavers had ended, few remained. Then as we humans continued to build bigger and bigger cities and shape Mother Earth for our own purposes, those in charge, the companies, once again began hunting the beaver—this time with the intention of eliminating them; too often had beavers disrupted progress. The resources of Mother Earth were dwindling, and no longer could these animals be tolerated. Sadly, they succeeded; beavers became extinct. Well, all but one, my children. Castor alone had eluded them. She was the very last of her kind. The Creator saw this and was saddened to see such great creatures completely destroyed, so the Creator gifted to Castor the ability to transform into any creature to better evade her hunters. Castor transformed into every animal she knew of, and she learned what it was like to live as each creature for a time, but still she did not feel safe from humankind. One day, she thought to transform herself into a human and, at last, found safety. She walked two legged among the humans, and she learned from them for many years, but Castor was still, in her heart, a beaver, and she longed for a companion. The Creator said, 'If you can promise to leave behind the greediness of your kind, I will use the power I gave you and create a mate for you, but you must take only from the land what you need, and never more.' Castor agreed and transformed into a beaver for the last time, and she found the mate promised her; the two built a home together. But it wasn't long before Castor forgot the lessons she'd learned. She forgot about her time as a mouse, her time as a deer, and her time as a wolf, and she and her mate—"

"Moushoum—south of the valley—two people approach," said Anna, a black-haired woman, who approached the group gathered under the oak. She carried a long, wooden spear.

"I am sorry young ones," said the Elder, standing up. "We will finish the story when I return."

Two others, Jonathon and Will, joined Thomas and Anna as they walked to the forested southern entrance, where they passed a group patrolling the way into the valley. Not long after, Thomas and the three others happened across the two strangers, a man and a woman; Thomas stepped forward and welcomed them.

"*Tawnshi kiya*. Hello and welcome."

The bearded stranger grabbed the rifle he carried over his shoulder and levelled it at them. The woman stepped back, raised her machete and said, "We don't mean any harm."

Thomas contemplated the two for a moment. "And we mean no harm to you."

The man, visibly weary from travel, shook his rifle at them. "Sorry if we don't take your word for it. It . . . it's a messed up world these days."

"Hehe. She's been 'messed up' for every one of the seventy-six years

I have known her."

"You know . . . I mean . . . since 'they' came. What . . . eight or nine years ago now? I can't even keep track anymore."

"It has been nine winters," said Thomas. He looked up at the low-hanging morning sun. " . . . soon to be ten."

The Elder pointed at each of his companions. "This is Jonathon, this is Anna, and this young buck here, well, his name is Will. I'm Thomas."

Still in her defensive posture, the woman said, "I'm Maria. That's Chris."

"We're hungry . . . if you have any food to spare," added Chris.

"We are happy to share our food." Thomas nodded to Jonathon, who set off back into the valley.

"May I approach and sit? The others will stay back. This old man needs to rest his tired knees."

Maria nodded. Thomas ambled toward the two and sat down on a log nearby. He motioned to them. "Please, join me."

They did; though their weapons remained at the ready.

"Where are you from?" asked Thomas.

"Portland," replied Chris.

"Vancouver," said Maria.

"What did you do before? Before 'they' came?" asked the Elder.

"Environmental research," said Maria. "You know, trying to save the world."

Chris smiled. "Insurance. Ha, what a joke that was—the singular worst job to have when the world blows up. In the first few days, everyone was looking to collect; there wasn't a dollar to be had. People continually threatened to kill us; well, at least until they realized money wasn't going to help them."

Maria nodded at this as Chris continued with his story. "It's ironic; you know, death threats actually saved my life. I fled Portland the day before it was destroyed. I drove north—as far as I could anyway. Then I walked along the highway until that went all to hell. 'They' were killing people; people were killing people. Seattle was the worst. I spent a few years trying to lay low on the outskirts of the city, scrounging for food. Couldn't stick your head up for long though. The bastards were herding people up like cows into pens. And then they . . . they . . . just vacuumed them up, alive and kickin', right into space. You could see them, thousands at a time, go up and up and up like . . . like gravity wasn't even a thing . . . until they were just . . . gone."

Chris stared at the ground. "I was lucky to get out of Seattle, and I just kept heading north. I figure we're in Canada, but whereabouts, I couldn't tell you. Do you know where we are? Which province even?"

Thomas smiled. He had lost a few teeth to old age in the past few years. "Hehe. Everything has purpose, Chris, and I suppose those artificial lines you speak of had theirs, but that time is gone."

"Yeah, I guess it is."

"Chris joined up with my group," said Maria. "Now there's just the two of us left. We run into others occasionally, but we don't stay; it's safer in small groups. We pick up small bits of news here and there."

"Yeah, a few weeks back we ran into a group of four who had heard that the leaders of all the largest countries are kept for entertainment. They say the President of the United States is naked in a cage somewhere and is forced to welcome each new group of invaders," said Chris.

"More of that irony you spoke of, eh?" said Thomas.

"I can see killing us to take our planet, but why the cruelty?" said Maria.

"This is nothing new. Our own history shows that even human colonizers thought of all Indigenous peoples as lesser beings, often treating them worse than they treated their own animals."

"True," agreed Maria.

"So, is it just the four of you?" asked Chris.

Thomas smiled. "There are nearly two hundred in our village."

"Two hundred? That's not possible," said Maria. "How have you survived? We haven't come across any groups of more than five or six people in over a year. Everyone's been wiped out."

"We live in harmony with the land," said Thomas. "Many years ago, long before 'they' came, I had gone back to the old ways, living off the land. I took only what I needed, and I gave thanks for all of it. I honoured the old ways—the ways taught to me by my grandfather. Others joined me, and over the years, more and more have come.

"But two hundred? You're asking for trouble," said Chris.

Jonathon returned with two carved wood bowls filled with salmon and corn.

"Thank you," said Chris, taking the bowl of food from Jonathon with one hand, keeping the other on his rifle.

"Yes, thank you," said Maria, taking the food offered.

Chris looked over at the rest of Thomas's companions. "Are you all Native American?"

Thomas grinned gap-toothed at this.

Maria shook her head.

Thomas spoke while Maria and Chris ate. "The First Peoples of Turtle Island were here tens of thousands of years before America or Canada, and they have now outlived them both. Just as they have outlived the names imposed upon them. I am Métis, what they once called 'half-breed', and many of us here are of First Peoples' heritage, but many are not. All are welcome; we are all related."

"But I still don't see how you've managed to avoid them," said Maria, pausing from gulping down food. "I mean, we're all living 'off the grid' now, and that hasn't stopped other groups, big and small, from being wiped out."

"Hmmm, yes, but there is more to it than abandoning laptops and cellphones," said the Elder. "We must live the old ways. We must respect the land. Most still do not understand this. We do not harvest more than our community can eat. When we hunt, we use all of the animal— nothing goes to waste. And most importantly, we've left all of the new ways behind. If you can accept this way of life, you are welcome to join us."

Chris and Maria handed their empty bowls to Jonathon, thanking him.

"So what you're saying is you want me to hand over my gun?" said Chris.

"No, we have no use for it. I'm asking you to destroy it."

"What? And if they do come, how would we defend ourselves? With spears? Ha."

"Chris, just listen," said Maria.

"I need this for protection," said Chris, clutching the rifle as he stood up. "If they come, I need this."

"They will only come if you keep it," said the Elder.

"That's ridiculous. How can they know I've even got it?"

"How could they know we were killing our planet? Did they hear her screams? Somehow they knew, and they came."

"What are you saying? That they came here to save Earth?" asked Maria.

"That's ridiculous!" said Chris. "They came to colonize Earth; they've destroyed every city, every satellite, every power station, every dam."

"But built none of their own. Why is that?" asked the Elder. "It is true; more come all the time, but many leave as well."

"How do you know this?" said Chris.

"I too hear things. And it is up to each of us to determine fact from falseness."

"Look, I'm not giving up my only means of protecting myself."

"And what happens when you run out of bullets, Chris? That day will come."

"We're headed way up north. We've heard there's a fort there that's heavily armoured; we're going to lay low with them. Build up some defences. Repopulate. It'll take many years, but we'll take back what's ours."

"Yours? Hmmm . . . yours to . . . to dominate? To shape as you see fit?"

"We just want to get things back to the way they were," said Maria.

"The 'way they were' was a world on the verge of collapse. Maria, you know the shape we were in—the shape Mother Earth was in. The extinction of so many animals. We cannot repeat those mistakes."

Maria didn't reply.

"It's better than a world controlled by hostile invaders," said Chris.

"The world we live in here is beautiful, plentiful, and peaceful."

"But for how long?" asked Maria.

"They have been—"

"Look." Chris interrupted the Elder. "You've just been lucky out here—too remote to worry about—yet. They'll come for you, you wait and see, they'll come!"

A momentary silence ensued—a silence abruptly broken when the two thanked the group again for the food and set off north. Maria looked back momentarily before the two disappeared into the dense woods.

"But . . . they've already been here," said Thomas.

Jonathon appeared by his Elder's side. "Uncle, should we have told them the 'others' came from the north when they came, and that we live in peace with them?"

"It would have done no good. They weren't going to listen. They weren't going to change."

When Thomas returned home with the others, he once again gathered the children together under the oak.

"Now, where was I?"

"Castor forgot her teachings," said several of them.

"Hehe. Right. Castor had forgotten what it was like to be one of the other animals. She had also forgotten the teachings she had learned as a human. But most importantly, she had forgotten her promise to the Creator. Castor and her mate found a wonderful stream and cut down many trees to build their home. Their home, in turn, blocked the stream, which then flooded a meadow, chasing the mice and the deer from the fields. But the beavers wanted a bigger home yet, so they cut down even more trees. This bigger home flooded a nearby forest, now leaving the wolves without a home. It did not take long for the humans to realize what had happened. First, they destroyed the cause of the flood— Castor's home. Then they killed Castor's mate and cornered Castor. She called out for the Creator's help, but she heard no reply. Castor was indeed the last of the beavers."

The children listened intently as Thomas finished the tale first told to him by his grandfather. The Elder smiled and raised his hands to them, lifting them up.

"All my relations," said Thomas.

Artwork by Leanna Raven Paul

Connie Fife
Cree

New Ways

now as a grown woman
i have passed through the brief solitudes
brought on by the changing of another season

the slow movement of shifting colours
and the loping arrival of winter
your absence has been replaced
by the warmth of full bellied poems
who have slept nestled against my spine
their tongues peeling back on old skin

i am trying to find new ways to live
original means by which to feel alive
the breathing in and out of a
politic by which to free a heart
that the stars have already caught in their throats

AUTHOR Bio's

Joanne Arnott

Joanne is a Métis/mixed-blood writer and editor, mother to six young people and author of eight books. Her first book, *Wiles of Girlhood*, won the League of Canadian Poets' Gerald Lampert Award (1992). Her most recent poetry titles are *Pensive & beyond* (Nomados 2019), *A Night for the Lady* (Ronsdale 2013), and *Halfling spring: an internet romance* (Kegedonce 2013). She co-edited a collection with Deanna Reader, Michelle Coupall, and Emalene Manuel, *Honouring the Strength of Indian Women: Plays, Stories, Poetry by Vera Manuel* (University of Manitoba Press, 2019). Joanne received the Vancouver Mayor's Arts Award for Literary Arts for 2017. She is currently the Poetry Mentor at SFU's The Writers Studio, and Poetry Editor for *Event* magazine.

Michael Calvert

Michael is a member of the Mid-Island Métis Nation. His poetry, fiction, and non-fiction have been published in various magazines. Michael won the Pat Bevan Award for fiction writing in 2012 and a Meadowlarks Award for a promising body of fiction work. His fiction piece "Flood Damage" placed second in the *In Our Own Aboriginal Voice* 2016 writing contest. This year, his short story "All My Relations" won first place for fiction in *In Our Own Aboriginal Voice 2*. Michael has taught in the Creative Writing & Journalism department at Vancouver Island University and currently teaches First Peoples Literature and Composition at Vancouver Island University.

Shauntelle Dick-Charleson

Born in Nanaimo, BC, Shauntelle is Lekwugen and Nuu-chah-nulth (Hesquiaht and Songhees). She is 16 years old and currently lives in Victoria, BC where she attends Reynolds Secondary and is enrolled in the soccer academy. Culture has always been a big part of Shauntelle's life. She was raised learning her mother's side of culture, and she loves listening and taking part in it. Her parents told her to always be truthful and respectful and she shares her truth through her poetry—she knows her truth needs to be heard.

Hank Charles

Hank is a member of the Lac La Ronge Indian Band in northern Saskatchewan. His band consists of six reserve communities that have gone through social upheaval as a result of colonization and residential schools. Writing, for Hank, is a way to release the trauma. It is a way to teach society about what happened. Land-based education has always been his interest, and he previously published an article on that topic, "Reconnecting with the Land: Embracing 'Nihithaway Pimatisiwin' as a basis for land-based education, healing, and reconciliation", *2018 – First Peoples Writing Undergraduate Journal – British Columbia.*

Jo Chrona

Jo is a member of the Ts'msyen Nation; her grandmother is from Kitsumkalum and her grandfather from Kitsegukla. She is Ganhada from the House of K'oom. Her father's family was of European descent. Jo has worked in the field of education for over twenty years teaching both youth and adults, developing curriculum, and writing resources. She is passionate about supporting a truly inclusive educational experience for all learners where honouring Indigenous voices and valuing Indigenous knowledge are valued. When not writing, Jo's creativity finds outlets in baking and painting, the products of which she loves to share with others.

Connie Fife

Connie Fife (1961– 2017) was a Cree poet and editor. A survivor of the 60s Scoop, Connie published three books of poetry, *Beneath the Naked Sun* (Sister Vision, 1992), *Speaking through Jagged Rock* (Broken Jaw, 1999), *Poems for a New World* (Ronsdale, 2001) and the anthology *The Color of Resistance: A contemporary collection of writing by Aboriginal women* (Sister Vision, 1993). In 2000, Connie received the one-time Prince and Princess Edward Prize in Aboriginal Literature, in recognition of her contribution both in Indigenous communities, and to Canada as a whole. This poetry was drawn from her unfinished collection, "Returned" (2001 – 2017).

Kevin Bear Henry

Bear is a Coast Salish multi-media artist who self identifies as two-spirited and trans femme. Bear is heavily inspired by culture, land, and language revitalization. For the past fifteen years, Bear has been rediscovering all aspects of their Hul'q'umi'num heritage, much of which is through the use of art expression such as photography, writing, and poetry. Bear is a social worker, prominent voice of land protection through art as a method of healing, and appreciates the opportunities afforded to them.

ILRP 100 class (Vancouver Island University) -The Indigenous Learning Recognition Portfolio course at Vancouver Island University is an exploration of Indigenous identity. Students build a portfolio through reflection of who they are, where they are from, where they are going and how they can give back to community. Students in the spring 2019 course also explored their collective voice through the creation of story. Members of the class brought ideas forward for the development of the story throughout the semester, with Hayden Taylor, Keandra Thompson, Quinn James, Joanna Harris, and Francis Guerrero weaving it all together in the last couple of weeks of class. Many extra hours were put in by these students to bring this story to its finalized version.

Charla Lewis

One still summer day, Charla was visiting her late grandmother's burial site in Swxwú7mesh; she was overcome with grief and guilt because for so long she hadn't understood her grandmother's ways. It wasn't until later that she came to understand how strong she was for surviving, day by day, in a world that didn't recognize her pain. As she knelt at her grandmother's burial site, a warm breeze wrapped itself around her, enveloping her; all grief and guilt seemed to melt from her. "It was my grandmother, I am certain of that—my spirit recognized her. I hope to honour her in these poems."

Natasha McCarthy

Natasha was born and raised in Nanaimo, BC by a strong, single mother of two. She grew very close with her aunt throughout her childhood, and after her traumatic passing, Natasha chose to walk away from her culture. Natasha struggled throughout high school, being told she would never amount to anything. In her early 20s, she met the love of her life and moved to Campbell River, BC. Her partner encouraged her to go back to school to pursue her dreams—she graduated on the Deans' list from the HCA program at NIC. She found happiness again, returned to her culture, and began writing.

Darlene McIntosh

Darlene's role as Elder encompasses an ever-expanding scope from protocols of traditional territorial welcoming of guests/people/meetings/special events: offerings of blessings and prayers, opening meetings and circles, acting as witness in meetings and tribunals as well as sitting on Aboriginal Advisory Committees. These demands are rising not only because of increasing protocols, but because of the wisdom and warmth that Darlene embraces through her gift of writing and being able to weave her insights into the purpose of the gathering, thus interconnecting people, purpose and spirit. Darlene's most vital role in the community is her contributions to education as the Cultural Advisor in the Aboriginal Resource Centre. Darlene has been a mainstay and fountain of support, teaching and leadership for students. She has helped them navigate their paths toward academic success. More importantly, Darlene has been the critical link throughout the wider network of the College of New Caledonia's quest toward indigenization and reconciliation. She is the educator, mediator, cultural advisor, and spiritual leader for staff, executive, faculty and, of course, students. Darlene's interconnectedness and love for Mother Earth grounds her in the reality of today. *Mussi*

Connie Merasty

Connie is a Fluent Cree speaker, Two Spirit human rights advocate. "I would eventually like to teach Cree in my community, encouraging aspiring writers to hone their craft, learning about traditional ceremonies and storytelling. I am inspired to write by other First Nations artists, such as Tomson Highway, Chrystos, Billy Merasty, Maria Campbell, and Jordan Wheeler. I grew up in a home with a wood stove and an outdoor toilet. I remember when all we spoke was Cree in our home. Our language needs to be taught and writers of the world can help bring this resurgence about in our communities. *Ekosani.*"

Sharai Mustatia

Sharai is a Métis-Cree/Romanian writer originally from Regina, SK. They are currently writing their first novel about the experience of coerced adoption within the Canadian-Indigenous socio-political landscape.

Sharai was invited to participate in the Indigenous Writers residency at Banff Centre For Creativity in 2013. Their writing has been published in the Indigenous anthology *Dreaming in Indian* (Annick Press, 2014) where it appeared alongside other emerging Indigenous artists and writers. Their writing and film photography is political, spiritual and deeply personal. Sharai values kindness as a radical act of compassion.

Myles Neufeld

Myles has been writing his entire life; it has been his one constant emotional support through life's struggles. He hopes to become a successful author who can begin writing manuscripts and fill the media with queer people of colour. Myles has been published multiple times by Polar Expression's Publishing, but he says to be published here is a great honour which doesn't go unnoticed. He is a proud queer, Indigenous author excited for what the future holds for him.

Jeremy Ratt

Jeremy is a Métis writer and artist with heritage from Peter Ballantyne's Cree Nation. His interest in storytelling sparked at an early age, to which he spent his time watching movies and reading comic books. As an English Honours student in high school, his passion was reflected through various short stories, short films, and poetry. On top of being a writer, Jeremy is an actor, having performed in various theatre productions, short films, and recorded voice over work. Jeremy resides in British Columbia, continuing to craft new art in hopes of bettering the image of Aboriginal people in media.

Skeena Reece

Skeena is a performance/visual artist based on Vancouver Island. She is grateful for her peer support as she raises two children and makes work to inspire others, and herself, as she heals.

Sheena Robinson

Sheena is a Heiltsuk woman who grew up in Vancouver, BC and discovered her love of reading and writing at an early age. Her inspiration comes from the various places she's lived along the northwest coast, including Bella Coola, Mayne Island, Nanaimo, and Bella Bella, where her family on her mom's side is from. She recently graduated from Vancouver Island University with a BA in First Nations Studies and Creative Writing. She's been published in VIU's *Portal* and *Incline* magazines, and is currently working on a young adult novel. In the writing contest component of this anthology, Sheena won second prize fiction for "Grey Skies" and second prize poetry for "Saving Cedar Saving Me." Sheena also recently made the longlist for the 2019 CBC Nonfiction Prize for "Identity Dreams."

Dennis Saddleman

Dennis was born in 1951 in Merritt, BC. He went to Kamloops Residential School for eleven years. He has struggled in life from sexual abuse, drugs, alcohol, hate, and violence. He has been clean and sober for thirty-eight years. He learned how to write—writing has been his passion for many years. His poems have helped him to travel to many places, like Edmonton, Winnipeg, Toronto, Ottawa, and Honolulu where he has been invited to share his poems and stories at universities, colleges, senior and elementary schools. His family and friends call him "Word Warrior."

Spencer Sheehan-Kalina

Spencer is a writer and artist who believes that stories, words, and art can change lives. He is a Fine Arts student at North Island College and currently lives in Courtenay, BC. He was born in Ottawa and is a member of the Métis Community of Maniwaki. Spencer has been previously published by Rebel Mountain Press in the anthology *In Our Own Aboriginal Voice* (2016), and the picture book *Nootka Sound in Harmony: Aboriginal Connections* (2019).

Maisyn Sock

Maisyn is a nineteen-year-old Mi'kmaq First Nations woman from the communities of Eskasoni, Nova Scotia and Elsipogtog, New Brunswick. She has a twin, Camryn, who inspires her. She has a big family which has led her to be very family oriented. She enjoys using writing as her way of release, taking all the emotion she feels and channelling it into her writing. She hopes to inspire the youth in her communities by taking these opportunities. She is thankful for the culture that shaped her into who she is.

Jerry Smaasslet

Originally from Fort Ware, BC, Jerry is a member of the Carrier Sikanni Nation. He served over 30 years of a life sentence in the Fraser Valley, before being released to the Circle of Eagles Halfway House. Writing gives Jerry balance, awareness, emotional freedom, and a strong bond with his inner child. He recently became a high school graduate which he hopes will inspire and encourage warriors, life-givers, and the wounded to carry on. He trusts the Creator, and his release to the Circle of Eagles Lodge has humbled him as he continues walking in the tradition. Jerry wishes to serve as a role model or advisor, helping those who seek a brighter side. This is Jerry's second publication. A portion of Jerry's story was previously published by Rebel Mountain Press in *In Our Own Aboriginal Voice* (2016). Jerry hopes that others, especially the young, can learn from his mistakes.

Joe Starr

Gya yu stees (Joe Starr, in Haisla) from Nanaimo, BC is a member of the Haisla First Nation in Bella Bella. He began to write about six years ago as therapy. He has self-published two books: *Nuyem Weaver*, a collection of short stories; and *NOSTA,* a Grade 4/5 chapter book that is set in Kitamaat and ends in Bella Bella. Joe has also been previously published in the anthology *In Our Own Aboriginal Voice* (Rebel Mountain Press, 2016), and he is a co-author of *We are all Connected: Haisla, Rivers and Salmon* (Strong Nations, 2017).

Michelle Sylliboy

Michelle, a L'nuk (Mi'kmaq) artist/author, was born in Boston, Massachusetts and raised on unceded territory in We'koqmaq Cape Breton. Arriving on the art scene in 1995, her Interdisciplinary art practice embodies some of her own life experiences which has led her to work with emerging and professional artists from all over Turtle Island. Michelle recently moved back to her territory after living and working on unceded Coast Salish territory for twenty-seven years. While in Vancouver, she learned to capture and intrigue the art community with her Interdisciplinary style of work. She gathers much of her inspiration from personal tales, the environment, and her L'nuk culture. PhD Candidate, Michelle is working on her Philosophy of Education Doctorate where she combines her artistic background and education by creating a L'nuk *Komqwejwi'kasikl* (Hieroglyphic) curriculum with L'nuk teachers and Elders in Cape Breton. Previous publications include *Kiskajeyi – I AM READY, a Hermeneutic exploration of Mi'kmaq Komqwejwi'kasikl poetry* (Rebel Mountain Press, *2019*).

Edōsdi /Judy Thompson

Edōsdi means 'someone who raises up children and pets'. Edōsdi's English name is Judy Thompson and she is a member of the Tahltan Nation. She is the Director of the Language Reclamation Department for her nation and is an Assistant Professor in Indigenous Education at the University of Victoria. Her passion is Indigenous language revitalization. Over the last three decades, she has been learning their language from her grandparents and other Tahltan Elders. She's made it a life goal to experience her people's ways of knowing, the worldview of our Ancestors, through their language. In the writing contest component of this anthology, Edōsdi won first prize poetry for "My Grandfather's Cherished Mittens."

Eliot White-Hill, Kwulasultun

Eliot is a member of the Snuneymuxw and descended from the Hupacasath people through his patrilineal grandmother, Joyce White. He recently graduated from Vancouver Island University's Bachelor of the Arts program with a major in Liberal Studies and a minor in Philosophy. He credits his lifelong love of reading and storytelling to his family upbringing; particularly to his mother, Ilse Hill, who is another voracious reader and a never-ending resource for suggestions, and his late great-grandmother, Dr. Ellen White,

Kwulasulwut, whose own storytelling and work to preserve Coast Salish culture and tradition has provided so much ground to stand on as a Coast Salish writer.

Jillian Wicks

Jillian is a full-time mother/wife and writes poetry as a hobby. She developed a strong interest in poetry in high school, with special thanks to a very influential English teacher. She keeps most of her poetry work private and personal. This is her first published submission, and she looks forward to sharing more of her work with others. Upon writing this poem, she realized it was meant to be shared. She hopes it inspires others to find their voice and strength as modern-day Indigenous persons.

John Williams

John is a Cree writer from George Gordon First Nation. He loves his cat, Edison. He was born in Saskatchewan and was lucky enough to spend half his life in Jasper, Alberta. The prairies and the mountains will always be in his writings. A spiritual connection with nature is a strong guiding force in John's life. John Williams is one of the most common names in the English-speaking world.

ARTIST Bio's

Phillip Joe

Phillip is a Salish artist from the Quwutsun Tribes reserve in Duncan BC on Vancouver Island. Phillip has been influenced by artists such as Edward Joe, Stuart Pagaduan, Joe Wilson, Manuel Salazar, Delmar Johnnie, and Art Thompson. He is interested in doing limited edition prints. His says his dream is to have these employment tools and share these gifts with his children and grandchildren, so they can also have tools to be self-sufficient and make their own income in their own time. His hobby is Native art, which he has been creating for thirty-one years. "I want to share a beautiful gift that I received from the Creator," he says. Phil's artwork is previously published in volume one of *In Our Own Aboriginal Voice*. If you are interested in Phil Joe's art, please contact him at email: philjoe74.pj@gmail.com

Sharai Mustatia
(see Author Bio's)

Leanna Raven Paul

Leanna's background is Anishinaabekwe. She lives in Vancouver, BC. Her work has also been published by Rebel Mountain Press in volume one of *In Our Own Aboriginal Voice* (2016). Leanna's interests are decolonization, learning, singing "off-key" in her car, trap line families, movies, and love.
To see more of Leannna's artwork, visit her website: rav3nz.com.

Jerry Smaasslet
(see Author Bio's)

Michelle Sylliboy
(see Author Bio's)

Niki Watts

Niki Watts is a Cree artist from rural Bella Coola, BC. Watts' remote upbringing and her Plains Cree heritage continues to inspire her work. Being born and raised in a rural community, she developed a close connection to nature and wildlife. Watts has displayed her work at the prestigious National Art Gallery of Canada in Ottawa and was in the top three in an art contest open to youth artists across Canada. In 2017 she was selected for the prestigious Hnatshyn Foundation's REVEAL Indigenous Art Award. Watts graduated with a Bachelors degree at Emily Carr University of Art & Design. She believes that art can be a catalyst for change and can be a voice for issues that need to be heard. For more about Niki's work see: nikiwattsartist.com

INDIGENOUS TITLES BY REBEL MOUNTAIN PRESS

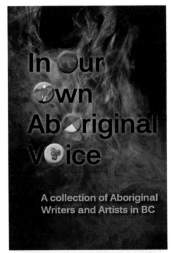

In Our On Aboriginal Voice:
A collection of Aboriginal Writers and Artists in BC

Authors: Michael Calvert, Mary-Ann Chevrier, Maryann Dick, Kevin Henry, Darlene McIntosh, Natalia Auger Nybida, Ry-Lee Pearson, Kirsten Sam, Spencer Sheehan-Kalina, Kris J Skinner, Jerry Smaaslet, Joe Starr.
Artists: Shelby Brown, Phil Joe, Evelyn Jones, Hailee Jones, Hanna Peters, Leanna Raven Paul, Carmen van Soest.
ISBN:978-0-9947302-4-4

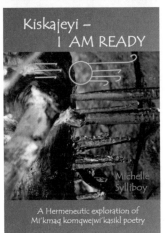

Kiskajeyi- I AM READY

This hieroglyphic poetry book is the first of its kind. Aboriginal author/artist Michelle Sylliboy blends her poetry, photography, and Mi'kmaq (L'nuk) hieroglyphic poetry in this unprecedented book. Hieroglyphic (komqwejwi'kasikl) symbols dominated the landscape of the seven districts of the L'nuk Nation prior to colonization.

Author/photographer: Michelle Sylliboy
Editor: Michael Calvert
ISBN: 978-1-7753019-2-9

Nootka Sound in Harmony:
Aboriginal Connections

Children's Picture Book (ages 3-8)

Author: Spencer Sheehan-Kalina
Illustrator: Kim Nixon
ISBN: 978-1-7753019-3-6

LGBTQ2 TITLES BY REBEL MOUNTAIN PRESS

LGBTQ2 Writers on Coming Out and Into Canada

Breaking Boundaries

An anthology of fiction, memoirs and poetry by LGBTQ2 writers (Canada-born, immigrated or refugee). The common thread throughout is that for LGBTQ2 people, Canada is the place to be.

Nominated for the 2019 GEORGE RYGA AWARD . The George Ryga Award is an annual literary prize for a B.C. writer who has achieved an outstanding degree of social awareness.

ISBN: 978-0-9947302-7-5

GHOST'S JOURNEY:
A Refugee Story

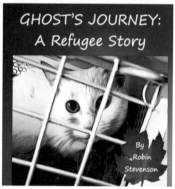

When Indonesia becomes an unsafe place for the LGBTQ+ community, it is no longer safe for Ghost (the cat) and her two dads to live there. As told through the eyes of Ghost, journey with them on their escape as they become refugees and find freedom in Canada

Author: Robin Stevenson
ISBN: 978-1-7753019-4-3

UPCOMING- MARCH 2020

DISABLED VOICES ANTHOLOGY

Written and illustrated by the disabled community about the disabled community, Disabled Voices is an international anthology collection of short story (both fiction and non-fiction), personal essay, poetry, and artwork. Featuring both new as well as established authors.
Editor: sb smith
ISBN: 978-1-7753019-5-0

REVIEWS: *IN OUR OWN ABORIGINAL VOICE 2*

"I pray that the artwork, the sharing of these stories brings healing to both the artists and those who engage with this collection. It contains a tsunami of pain but does not leave you there. There is medicine in these stories, stories that could only be told by those who lived to tell. Some still seek restitution, long for healing, and to bring home the bones of their ancestors. All are courageous in the telling." ~ Jónina Kirton, Métis/Icelandic poet, author of *An Honest Woman* (Talonbooks, 2018)

"Words, woven threads of tumultuous, sometimes distant, memories that tie us together. Mixed with sinuous, golden threads of distant, sometimes extant threads of sunlight that hold dreams, hope, love, safe homes and where we embrace our Creator. Our strength in gentle words, sometimes warrior words, ties us together in this complex collection of words that reflect us all." ~ Terri Mack, Da'naxda'xw Awaetlala Nation, author of the *Raven Series* and owner of Strong Nations Books

"This ongoing commitment to further the remarkable growth of Indigenous literature can only be applauded." ~ Alan Twigg, author of *Aboriginality: The Literary Origins of British Columbia, Vol. 2* (Ronsdale, 2005)

"These voices are precious and beautiful. Mahsi cho to each of them singing the world to a brighter place. Mahsi cho to them. Mahsi cho to their families. Mahsi cho to their ancestors and mahsi cho to a richer world because of their courage and bravery. I am grateful and humbled and inspired." - Richard Van Camp, Dogrib (Tlicho) Nation, author of *Moccasin Square Gardens* (Douglas and McIntyre, 2019)

"The poets and short-story writers who contributed here for our enjoyment leave us with the message that you are known; someone knows you exist, "I no longer must fear that I am alone." - Edmund Metatawabin, Former Chief of Fort Albany First Nation, author of *Up Ghost River: a Chief's journey through the turbulent waters of Native history* (Penguin Random House, 2015)